BUDHOO
AND OTHER SHORT STORIES

NAUMAN AFZAL

AURAQ
PUBLICATIONS

Printed: September, 2023
Edition: 1st
ISBN: 978-969-749-251-0
Price: Rs 1400 PKR, $10 US

Cover Art: @fatimabilalparacha
Cover Design: @asmacreatex
Illustrations: @thedarkersideof.me

www.auraqpublications.com | raabta@auraqpublications.com
@AuraqPublications | @AuraqBooks | +92-300-0571-530
Printed and Bound by *Passive Printers* - www.passiveprinters.com

DEDICATED TO MY FATHER

TESTIMONIALS

I had the pleasure of reading the compilation written by Mr. Nauman Afzal as Mudslinging. It was well-written and well-thought. It kind of gave me the feeling as if I'm reading some classic author like Mumtaz Mufti. Excited for his new book.

~Maleeha Zia Khan: @wordsofMIA

***

This book is based on everyday life experiences and observations. The author puts light on matters that happen regularly, that we encounter daily; but we never ponder upon them or speak up about them. This is sad but a reality and we're so used to it that we consider such things as normal. This book contains some significant lessons and we need to learn from them. The writing is simple, the stories are ordinary and that's what makes this book extraordinary. Mr. Nouman has a unique way of explaining the ills of our society in a very neutral and light tone. He's a phenomenal writer and I'd love to read more of his books as this one is outstanding! All the best for your future, may you succeed tremendously.

~Noorie Hassan @ thebookgeek1

***

Fascinating short stories with incredibly penned the common conflicts and how we can stand for it. Interesting yet amusing.

~Khulood Abdul Hadi from khulogophile_reads

***

Nauman Afzal's debut book - Mudslinging- has been edifying. He has left no stone unturned in depicting a realistic picture of our debauched society and thus with morals to inculcate, and makes one look inward. The employment of his language flows effortlessly like a brook. Simple and Sophisticated.

~Syeda Laluna @syedalaluna

***

Sir Nauman is such a flawless writer. His pen writes what every man sees but tends to neglect. He has the true observation of mishaps happening around and has a devotion to bring change. ~@literarylifeof_kaz

***

I am thrilled to express my heartfelt appreciation for Nauman Afzal, who is a very knowledgeable person, dedicated vlogger, an excellent writer, and a very humble human being. The impact of his writing extends far beyond the pages of his book, which becomes a true inspiration for aspiring writers and avid readers. His power of storytelling in his first book has inspired countless individuals including myself. No doubt his work will continue to inspire and enchant the generations to come. Get ready to be mesmerized, inspired, and stirred by the outstanding work of his upcoming masterpiece.

~Shakeel Ahmad. https://shakeelx.com

***

It is difficult to overstate just how fantastic and realistic a short story author Mr. Nauman Munir Afzal is. His collection of short stories is full of amazing portraits of a society rife with dishonesty, unethical behaviour, sarcasm, and a variety of other genres. The relatively harmless tales under the heading "Mudslinging" communicate honestly and plainly about society's problems in a way that is simple to understand. It is a wonderful literary achievement when you cry when reading about anarchies but also laugh while reading caustic descriptions of humorous events. You will be persuaded by the author's warmth and sensitivity for all the right reasons. My plan is to stick with series as I enjoyed every word of its initial two editions and fascinated the character presentation of the author ~(Twitter: @adnankhaniiui)

***

This collection of short stories provides an insight on prevailing social evils and makes me think about where we lie as a society. We, as a nation, are morally deteriorated and our society is heading to a dead end because of those immoral values we have adopted. Nauman afzal sahib has explained these social evils in such an effective way that it stops the readers for a while and makes them think about the scenarios. These short stories are light read yet really really thought provoking. Shahzina Shafi. ~@shahzinashafiaasi

***

I am delighted to share my testimonial for Mudslinging and Other Short Stories. As an avid reader, I was captivated by the stories that featured day to day instances rife with literary gems. Each story is crafted with remarkable skill and depth. The sincerity and authenticity is striking. The profound truth echoed in the stories pulled me into a world that felt vividly real. The struggles, triumphs and journeys of the characters resonated deeply with me. The brevity of the stories is a testament to the author's ability to capture the essence of a moment. I wholeheartedly recommend my father's short story book to any reader seeking an immersive and thought-provoking literary experience. It is a testament to his talent as a storyteller and his ability to craft narratives that resonate on a profound level. I feel privileged to have embarked on this literary journey through his book and eagerly await his future endeavors. ~Fatima Bilal Paracha

***

Nauman is a sensitive and deep thinker with vibrant expressions as a writer.......His understanding of complex human psyche and delicate structure of prevalent social fabric are uniquely insightful and thought provoking.....I would highly recommend reading of his upcoming 2nd book for an enthralling and deeply enriching experience. ~@danigem123

***

I had the pleasure of reading Sir Nauman's first book and was blown away by his talent. Now, with his second book on the way, I can't wait to see what he has in store for us. I have no doubt it will be just as amazing as his first." Sir Nauman Afzal" writing style is truly unique and captivating. I can confidently say that it is even better than his first. The characters are well-developed, the plot is engaging, and the writing is simply beautiful. I highly recommend this book to anyone looking for a great read. ~Erum Shamsi

***

Nauman Munir adeptly strums the strings in his new book. The notes ensuing are the sounds of humanity we hear all day, symphonies of angst, greed and treachery playing along love, loyalty and kindness. The tales are from mundane life – very relatable, and strike a chord of recognition in every reader's mind.

I am wondering what will play next? I am sure it will have enthralling and resounding notes as did "Mudslinging". Anticipating to understand my humanity better with the coming read. ~ Rubina Farooq

***

Mudslinging and other short Stories" by Nauman Afzal is a bouquet containing different issues (social and moral), harsh realities of life, romance and some light heartedness. The writer controlled the pace of the writing. The characters are very deeply described and colorful. The best part of the book is that it teaches readers that they have to seize the moment because you never know when life will end. My favorite story was, The Lonely Man. It also shows us that we have to embrace the pain that comes with being alive. My favorite lines from the story are, "There are two kinds of pain, one is physical and the other emotional. One can deal with physical pain, but there is no cure for emotional pain. ~ Faryal Waleed.

***

Nauman Afzal, author of Mudslinging and Other Short Stories, is an accomplished and versatile writer. His stories depict the social evils practiced in our Pakistani society. He has a keen eye for detail and writes with neutrality, wit, and irony, exposing the hypocrisy, corruption, and injustice that lurk behind the doors. ~Seemeen Khan Yousufzai, Author

***

Pakistani literature scene is witnessing the rise of an author who has no shame in writing about the real culture of Pakistanis. This is amazing because we are living in an era where freedom of speech has been shunned on all levels. Nauman is a courageous man & his stories are work of art but moreover, a work of promising observance. ~Salar Arif

Graphic Designer, Published Writer, Poet

Insta: @sentimental.virgo

PREFACE

Hello! When I wrote "Mudslinging and other short stories", I was skeptical about the feedback I was going to get. But then only after a few reviews I started getting encouragement which only increased with time. A few sales, a few PR book tours, and a few international sales later, the reviews kept getting more positive, on Instagram and on Google Goodreads. A year later people actually started asking me about my next book! Now that was some encouragement, I could never imagine people would actually ask me about my next book. Though frankly I never stopped writing after "Mudslinging" but the routine was haphazard and I wasn't very consistent in writing. But then when more people asked me, I decided to get serious and so I wrote some more and I am still writing. One of the problems I always face is deciding on when to stop? I wanted to do twenty stories in the second book, but then I decided to stop after thirteen stories. The rest would come later in another book, God willing.

So here we are today, with my second book titled, "Budhoo and other short stories" finally published. Only this time I have decided to add a different twist to the stories. I decided to write about domestic issues, as I kept writing the ideas kept coming, I experimented more and the results are here for you to read. Why not add a love story, how about some daydreaming, backstabbing, harassment issues, a story about a soldier perhaps? I must say for me writing is like therapy, and it works best when I am agitated and in a bad state.

I am grateful to a lot of people for their suggestions and ideas. Sarah my wife has been a great support always, Fatimah for designing the catchy cover photo and for proofreading the manuscript in record time, Ahmed and Ibrahim for their words of encouragement, Bilal Paracha for his support, Adnan Yousafzai for the wonderful ideas, Imran Zahoor for suggesting catchy titles on which at least one of the stories is based. Uncle Faqir Ahmed Paracha for asking me about my next book each and everytime we met or spoke, believe me, this helped a lot. Thank you to Sanober Zulfiqar for voluntarily proofreading and correcting the mistakes. Attiya Mudassir for proofreading, correcting mistakes and running AI software and punctuating the whole book. (I must confess I am really bad at punctuation).

Asma Anjum for designing the cover over and over again. There were times when I thought she would give up, but the digital artist went an extra mile each and every time, understood the requirement and reworked the cover. She also made valuable suggestions, besides having a busy schedule studying and sitting for her CSS exams. A big thanks to my dear friend Humayun for making the sketches for the stories, and for allowing me to use some of them from his Blog, I am sure he won't sue me someday for copyrights, lol. Nasreen Ghori has been a great support and volunteered to proofread the book. I am grateful to all of you.

I am also grateful to all my readers for the encouragement, for sparing the time and writing reviews. Each and every review has pushed me to go on and that is exactly what I did. I am happy that my book has been bought and read in the UK, US, Dubai, Bangladesh, Canada, India and Germany. I am already working on the third book. And once again thank you for your support and kind words. I surely do hope you enjoy the stories. Waiting to hear from my readers. Kind Regards,

Nauman Afzal

Rawalpindi, 28th July 2023

CONTENTS

BUDHOO

Zain Ibrar Shah was in the prime of his youth when he joined the District Management Group after having successfully cleared his CSS exams, interviews and mandatory training. At 26, the tall, handsome officer was posted as an SO in the Cabinet Division. Zain was from a feudal background, and his early schooling in Lahore had groomed him. He was privileged to have rubbed his shoulders with sons of bureaucrats, politicians and generals at the prestigious Aitchison College. The "tall, lanky fellow," as they called Zain, was equally good at studies and sports. Having passed his class with outstanding grades, Zain got College colors in Hockey, Athletics and Tennis. He was a good orator, an avid book reader and an able writer. He had the makings of a successful man from the very beginning. Then Tania came into his life, and the handsome Zain fell head over heels in love with the Kinnaird graduate, the daughter of a local businessman, just three years his junior. She was very pretty, with long dark hair flowing down her shoulders, fair-colored skin and a face like a doll. Best of all were those small dimples in her cheeks, which suddenly appeared when she smiled and for which Zain fell the first time he saw her. They fell in love in a matter of hours, took oaths of fidelity, never parted in a week, and were married two years later. His good education, feudal background, and handsome income from his vast lands gave him an air of superiority, and with these qualities, he excelled in his profession. Every new assignment brought him accolades and promotions. Zain Ibrar Shah excelled in his profession in the following years, aided by his feudal background and a supportive wife. Years later, he got promoted to the coveted rank of Additional Secretary, normally called the AS.

One hot and humid July morning, there was a lot of commotion in the Cabinet Division as the new AS sahib was going to take charge, and the staff had heard a lot about him from different sources. He was known to be honest, upright, tough and demanding but with a compassionate heart. People who worked hard weren't much worried about it, but the dodgers were apprehensive and, incidentally, were huge in numbers, which explained the sad state of things as they stood. His Personal Secretary had worked in advance and chosen the best staff for his office. The most efficient telephone operator was selected, the best clerks were fished out, and the finest driver was appointed. The office was whitewashed; fresh flowers were placed, the toilet was cleaned, and everything was near perfect, except for his Naib Qasid. The previous Naib Qasid had retired after reaching the age of superannuation and was now relaxing at his home in the village. A new man had to be found fast, and he had to be efficient. They asked around for people, but none could be found, the lazy ones preferred to stay away, and the efficient ones were already doing duty with other officers. It took the PS quite some time and effort to look for a suitable Naib Qasid. Finally, after the intervention of the

Joint Secretary Admin, a suitable man was found who was known to be straight as an arrow, efficient, hardworking, and one who knew his job, which of course, was rare. His name was Ghafoor Ahmed, and his colleagues called him Ghafoora. When the PS called him for an interview, he was somewhat surprised; the man wore spotlessly clean clothes, White Shalwar Kameez, a black waistcoat and black sandals. He had had a fresh haircut; his hair was oiled and combed, he wore a light oil-based perfume, had an old wristwatch on, and a pen in his left waistcoat pocket. The man spoke haltingly, but when asked about the location of various offices, the file work, his ability to make tea, and his knowledge about all things necessary, the PS was impressed. Ghafoora was perfect in every sense except that he had little experience as a Naib Qasid with senior officers. So Ghafoora was appointed as the AS Sahib's Naib Qasid, and the office order was typed and sent to all sections and wings. And with that, the PS finally heaved a sigh of relief.

On that hot and humid day in July, a little after 11 am, the new AS Zain Ibrar Shah walked into his office. He was received by the Joint Secretary, normally called the JS. After exchanging pleasantries, he was introduced to his staff by the JS, which included the young and smart SO Saima Gulfam, who took an immediate liking to the tall and lanky AS. Next up was the dark-skinned and exceedingly fat Deputy Secretary or DS named Meher Jan, who despised all those in more powerful positions than himself, who knew how to play his cards well and was known to use sugar-coated words, always. Finally, he was introduced to PS Humayun Khan, the clerks and Ghafoor Ahmed, aka Ghafoora. The AS briefly spoke to all of them and then went to have a cup of tea with the Cabinet Secretary. Hence, the first day was consumed with introductions and briefs and presentations. He was told they had lots of work to do and that the Cabinet Division was heavily overworked, and he told them about his life, career, and principles and that he was the one who always called a spade a spade and believed in setting things right. Years of working with the bureaucracy had given him an air of superiority to the extent that he thought or had started believing he was the smartest. He had that special quality with the spoken and written word, which, combined with his good education, persona, demeanor, connections and feudal background, made him stand out amongst his colleagues, subordinates and seniors. His perfect sense of dressing up, of wearing matching three pieces suits, Rolex watches, Waterman pens included, bracelets, branded shoes and the choicest of perfumes, added to his persona and the men and women around him were in awe because of this, save for one odd suave politician or bureaucrat whom he preferred to ignore, and they often reciprocated in similar ways. The man was known to have his way, in the office, at home and with friends. He was, or so he believed, perfect in every sense of the word.

The AS got down to work from day one, sparing no one and no effort in doing his job to the best of his abilities. He was destined to outshine everyone, excel and rise to the ranks of powerful Secretary and, after that, land a job at the UN or an ambassadorship somewhere in the West, most likely the US or UK. These were his secret plans which he shared with no one. Of all his staff, he found Ghafoora the most efficient, but then there was something odd about him. Ghafoora was always dressed in spotlessly clean clothes, always on time, very efficient and understood the requirements of his boss. If the AS wanted his cup of tea first thing in the morning, it was Ghafoora who gave him a hot steaming cup, be it summer or winter, just as he walked into his office. If anything, the AS Zain Shah was ever grateful to him; it was for that early morning cup of tea. When a special file meant for the "eyes of the Cabinet Secretary " or some senior person or even the politicians was to be handled, it was Ghafoora who was entrusted to do it. When it was pack-up time, Ghaffora would make sure that his boss's tracksuit, running shoes and even his smartwatch were laid out for him to change and go straight to the Islamabad Club gym for his daily workout. The AS often wondered how anyone could be so smart and efficient. Therefore, he regularly rewarded Ghafoora with sweet words of praise and small gifts whenever he was overcome by his efficiency. Despite all the good, there was still something off about Ghafoora that Zain Shah could sense but could not comprehend or quantify. With time, Ghafoora won his master's trust. According to the information, he was just a middle school pass, which would mean he was just literate enough to read and write perhaps a few words in his Urdu, although Ghafoora, who spoke with a lisp, preferred to converse in Punjabi, which he often did. There were times when Ghafoora would be silent, sometimes for weeks, but then he was just as efficient. Not a minute late, never on vacation, he was known never to have a day off. He was, in some ways, unexplainable when it came to defining his personality. But the AS and his staff grew fond of him; in some ways, it reminded him of the famous Tom Hanks movie Forrest Gump; Ghafoora was in many ways similar to Forrest Gump.

Days passed into weeks, and weeks into months. The AS and Ghafoora got along well. One day, when the AS came to his office after a hectic meeting and found

Ghafoora holding the AS Sahib's iPad in his hands, looking at it intently as if he was trying to figure out how it worked. The AS and Ghafoora exchanged looks; for a moment, AS lost his cool and was about to give him a good dressing down, but then he had known Ghafoora for almost a year and found him very reliable and loyal. Upon asking, Ghafoora kept quiet for a while and said, *"Sir bohat acha lagta hai yeh mobile mujhe"*. The AS said to him, *"Oye Budhoo, tum kiya jano yeh kiya cheez hai?"* Of course, the iPad had password protection, and he was at peace that his data was safe, but still he just smiled and got busy with his work. How could, he wondered, an uneducated man operate or perhaps even try to use an iPad, but then the AS got busy with his work.

However, the word "Budhoo" got around the offices and corridors of the Cabinet Division that day, and everyone in the lower staff had a hearty laugh at the new title given to that odd man, whom they called Ghafoora, whom they now started calling Budhoo. In one of those light and pleasing moments, the PS told the AS, Zain Shah, that Ghafoora was now being called Budhoo by everyone, at which the AS just smiled. A few days later, the PS got a call on his intercom asking him to send in "Budhoo" he immediately told Ghafoora to go to the AS Sahib's office, and they all had a big laugh. Ghafoora was now officially Budhoo, and everyone knew about it; even Ghafoora did not mind it. He just accepted it with a straight face. After a few days, Budhoo did not come to the office. It was rare, and none of the staff or the AS had a clue about his whereabouts or why he wasn't coming to the office. Even after inquiring around, no one knew anything about him. Since he had no mobile phone, no one could call him. Budhoo came to the office after being absent for three days. When he was called by the PS and the AS, he told them he wasn't well, and since he did not have a mobile phone, he could not inform them. That was rare but quite understandable; therefore, Budhoo was pardoned, his absence period was converted into casual leave, and life resumed as usual.

And then a few weeks later, when the AS came to his office from yet another meeting, he found Budhoo sitting in his huge revolving leather chair, enjoying a swing. At that moment, the AS Zain Shah lost his cool and gave him a good dressing down. Not only that, but he also called his PS and the rest of the staff and told them things that no one wanted to hear. He chided them for being casual and especially Budhoo for acting childish and immature. When asked, Budhoo replied, *"Sir jhula lene ka dil ker raha tha."* The AS was aghast; he looked at Budhoo, with the rest of the staff standing in his office and gave him a final warning, but a while later, he beamed a smile at them and started laughing. He could not comprehend how a low-ranking man like Budhoo could do something so stupid as to sit in his boss's chair. He found no parallels in comparing himself with Budhoo and hence decided that a man of his IQ must be stupid enough to do something like that, and he, the AS Zain Iqbal Shah, should act maturely and brush it off. And so the matter was forgotten.

One particularly windy and cold December day, when the AS came to his office, he found the room heated, his files in order, his cell phone fully charged, the iPad on its cradle, his laptop clean and tidy, a hot steaming cup of tea waiting for him and Budhoo standing with a smile on his face. The AS was impressed; he was impressed because Budhoo, he thought, had realized his mistakes of the past few days and, to make up for them, had acted in the best possible way. Being pleased beyond words, the AS asked him if he wanted anything, a gift or a favor perhaps, to which Budhoo smiled and pointed towards the Waterman pen in the AS Sahib's front pocket. The AS was a little taken aback; how could he give this pen to a Naib Qasid who was illiterate, well, almost and would find no use for the pen anyway. But then, being the clever and cunning man he was, he told Budhoo that the pen was a gift from a dear friend, which was a lie and that he could not give him that particular pen but would instead give him another one.

Even so, as a token of his appreciation, he put the costly Waterman pen in Budhoo's front pocket and took his photograph, which he later got printed, framed and gifted to Budhoo along with a cheap pen that he got through his PS. Budhoo was very happy that day, he visited all the offices in the whole building and being the simple man that he was, he showed the photo and the pen to everyone. And they were cunning and not as simple as Budhoo, laughed and made fun of him since they knew that Budhoo had been had by the AS Sahib. On the other hand, the AS Sahib was, of course, happy to have gotten himself off the hook.

A few days later, again, Budhoo did not come to the office for four days at a stretch, and it was presumed that he was unwell and absent. It again proved to be true, and so Budhoo was pardoned, and his absence again converted to casual leave. So things went smoothly for another few weeks, but then, as was wont to happen, Budhoo did something the AS found completely unacceptable. One day, Budhoo was found sitting on the sofa in the AS's office while in his absence, watching the BBC news channel. Again the matter was inquired, and it was told that Budhoo found the new girl with the golden hair attractive and was watching her. After all, Budhoo was unpredictable, and being the simple village person he was, his explanation was found acceptable yet again. The AS had grown fond of him; he was an interesting chap, efficient, punctual and loyal, but of course, in some ways unpredictable. Then again, the AS liked simple and stupid men because they made him appear intelligent and important and gave him an air of superiority. Hence all matters related to stupid men were forgotten, and those that were, in fact, smart and intelligent were made to look stupid and unintelligent because that's how things worked with him.

The AS had played his cards well until one day; he got his transfer orders for a coveted appointment in Punjab. He was being sent as Chief Secretary of Punjab. He would be the King or perhaps in the King's party; that is what the transfer order meant. He hurriedly planned to leave Islamabad for Lahore, the city he loved most. Eventually, a small farewell was arranged for him by his staff, but the worthy Secretary sahib delayed his departure on one pretext or another. He was instead sent to Japan for a week to attend an important meeting which he gladly accepted. Lahore could wait; Japan was more important for now. After a week, when the AS Zain Iqbal Shah returned from Japan and joined the office, he was again informed about Budhoo's absence by the PS. This wasn't odd at all since he had been absent on previous occasions as well. Although this time, he had been missing for a full week. Then another week passed, and there was no sign of Budhoo, so the PS, having been called by AS Sahib, sent a man to Budhoo's village and found his house locked and Budhoo's whereabouts unknown. The matter was reported to the JS Administration, who decided to write to the Police and ask them to inquire into the circumstances; Budhoo, after all, was a trusted Government employee in a very important office of the Government of Pakistan. An office that was at the center of all Government activity and hence of prime importance.

The next day, AS Zain Iqbal Shah got his orders to leave for Lahore. After having briefed his boss about his visit to Japan, he came to his office one last time and told his PS to pack his personal belongings. He asked for a cup of tea which was deftly provided to him, but it wasn't the taste that he had gotten used to, the one which Budhoo used to make. He actually missed Budhoo that day. Just before leaving, he heard a small email notification sound on his MacBook Air. What the hell, he thought; why was he supposed to check his email on his last day? But then, out of habit, he clicked on the email and started reading it, which was written in impeccable English.....

Dear Sir,

Adaab, I hope you are fine and in good health. I heard the news about your posting through my "friends". In fact, I knew about it for a long time, but of course, I could not tell you for reasons of secrecy. I just wanted to say that working with you was a great pleasure and honor for me. There were times when I thought you were very intelligent and smart, but after spending some time with you, I realized you were just as much stupid as the rest of the people around you. Please don't mind my saying this, but while the others knew they were unintelligent and stupid, they did not pose to be intelligent, while in your case, it was the other way around. Truth be told, you have survived and always excelled because of your persona and connections. You have always been a conformist, and that alone, perhaps, is why you have been so successful. Anyways, I just wanted to wish you well and tell you to keep on doing this on your next assignment, and hopefully soon, one day, you will make it big.

Allah Hafiz.

Yours Sincerely, Budhoo.

P.S. Please take a look at my latest picture in the attached file.

AS Zain Shah read the email twice, then read the sender's name; it had been sent by someone named Daniyal Azhar. When he clicked on the attached file, he saw a handsome man smartly dressed in trousers and a shirt with a beautiful woman in his arms. Upon closer inspection, it was Budhoo, and the pen the AS Zain Shah had gifted him was in his shirt pocket. Next to the photo was a handwritten note that read, "Aray Budhoo! all your files are safe with me, if you don't speak, I won't speak. Now you tell me who is the real Budhoo". When he saw the background, it was the unmistakable India Gate in Delhi. And that is when everything became clear to the mighty AS Zain Iqbal Shah, a fact that he had never known before. And so, he deleted the email, closed his laptop and left for his home.

CHAI PEEYO GI?

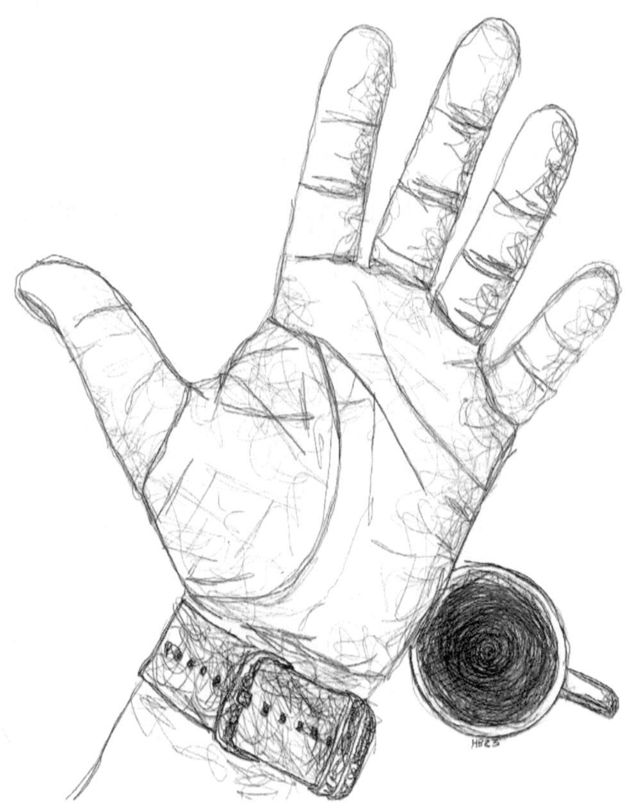

When my Abba passed away, I was in the final year of my BBA. Exams were almost over, and I contemplated applying for a job immediately after the exams. But that was not to be. Since I was the eldest, I had to take measures to run the house as Amma was mostly unwell.

Being less educated and a housewife all her life, she did not know how to make a living. She had, however, provided the best possible care to all her kids, that is me, Saira, my younger brother Noshad who will be fourteen soon and my younger sister Tooba who is ten. Sometimes, I used to wonder about the huge gap between us. Then, Amma once told me that I had a twin brother Yousaf who died when we were just six months old. Three years later, another baby boy, unfortunately, went into God's mercy upon birth. That explains the gap between me and my younger siblings. So, right after the exams, I applied for my transcript and, upon receiving it, made a CV and started applying for jobs. I was always a top scorer and had high expectations based on this. Besides, I was confident as I knew how to carry myself and would do my best if provided with an opportunity. After getting all the information about the job engines etc. I applied to all the advertisements and waited for a response. A few weeks passed, then a month, then another and finally, after three months, I just thought about giving up. Abba had worked all his life in a private construction firm. He had been an accountant there. The company did good business but did not have a good plan for the employees, due to which we got a meager sum of money which was barely enough for us. That, including some savings which my mother had, were enough to let us get by for a few months, at best. Life isn't easy nowadays; the cost of all commodities is sky-high. Then there are electricity bills, gas bills, school fees, transportation fees, and even food items are being sold at exorbitant prices. Even so, against all odds, we survived; in fact, we did a fine job under the given circumstances. But then, who has seen the future?

Soon things started getting difficult for us. Amma spoke to the local grocery shop owner, and after that, he used to loan us items which we paid for in small installments. But buying on credit had its disadvantages, as my siblings started getting petty things, thus increasing the bill enormously. Eventually, Amma put an end to it. And then, one day, as if things weren't difficult already, we received a huge property tax notice. To my mother's knowledge, we had never received a property tax notice. We did not know what to do because when my Abba was alive, he handled all such matters, and we rarely knew about these things. Then I, and Amma went to our neighbor Mr. Shamsi Sahib's house to seek guidance. Shamsi sb was a kind man; he told us that widows were exempted from paying property tax, but we would have to file papers. Thankfully, he handled the matter for us and saved us from many difficulties. It had now been almost six months, and I had not received a single reply from any of the places where I had applied for a job. On my insistence, Amma went to see Mr. Shamsi's wife and asked her to help us.

Mr. Shamsi was PS to an important Government Officer in a very senior position, and I was hopeful that he would help us. Except for him, we did not know anyone because Abba was the most successful or, perhaps you could say, well-established in our immediate family. Other than that, we had few close relatives, and even they never bothered to ask about our well-being or offer any help to us. Such are the wily ways of this world. When a man of no means dies, they all forget him soon. Mr. Shamsi promised to help us and asked for a copy of my CV. And then again, the wait started…

A few weeks later, around midday, I got my first call from an advertising company that wanted to interview me. I was very excited and prepared well for the interview. I searched the Internet for the FAQs by the HR people, what to say, what not to say, how to dress up, how to speak etc. etc. And so, on the appointed day, I walked into the office of TK Advertisement Agency located in an upscale area of the city. My mother was persistent in accompanying me, but I forbade her. So off I went in a rickshaw for my first-ever interview. A smartly dressed girl at the reception told me to sit in the waiting area. Full of optimism, I waited and then waited and waited some more.

After a good three hours, the same girl came and told me that the Boss was busy and would not be able to see me that day. I was shattered and, with a long face, hired a rickshaw and went home. When I saw my mother, I hugged her and burst into tears. She consoled me, served me lunch and told me to go to sleep. Three days later, they called me again, but this time, the Boss, or whoever he was, interviewed me. He was an intelligent-looking man who spoke as if practicing speech therapy, but of course, his words carried weight.

Along with him, there were two more men in the room. One of them was a middle-aged man with graying hair, and the other was just as old or young looking as the so-called Boss, and there was a lady whom they introduced to me as Ms. Ayesha. They asked me about my background, parents, and family and why I wanted to join an advertising company. They briefed me about the company ethics and policies and asked if I had any prior experience. Whenever the aged man spoke to me, I got nervous as he had this peculiar way of looking at me, which made me conscious of myself. He would ask me a question looking straight into my eyes, then shift his gaze to my feet. Suddenly after that, he would look at my bosom and then again at my face. He had this veiled sort of smile on his lips all the time. It was as though he wasn't interviewing but humiliating me.

Anyways, the interview lasted thirty minutes, but to me, it felt like hours. The aged man had made me extremely uneasy. Finally, Ms. Ayesha took me aside and told me I wasn't a potential candidate for the job. Still, since I had a recommendation from a very high place, I was being considered for this job, and I was to wait a little more for formal orders, which I would get soon. I returned home with a hotchpotch of feelings, unsure if I would get the job. After my father's death, I had lost all confidence. I started believing most of the time that only bad things would happen. It was a hopeless kind of feeling that I always had. I strongly believe there are two Sairas in me, the optimistic and good and the pessimistic and bad. Both of them are in a state of conflict with each other. Mostly, the bad one wins, but sometimes the good one overpowers the bad one. That, perhaps, is the reason why I am alive today.

Three days later, I received my offer letter and a contract document, which I promptly signed and delivered at the reception of the advertising company. Lo and behold, a week later, I received my appointment letter, and the next day, a Tuesday, I joined the office in the marketing section. Ms. Ayesha took me for a tour of the facility; well, there wasn't much of a facility. It consisted of five rooms, excluding the Boss's office, a small kitchen, a store and two washrooms! One for the ladies and the other for the gents. We had six female members on our staff, and the rest were male. It was a nice small office with a close-knit group of people, or so I thought. I got familiar with the people in the marketing section; there was Waseem, who, like me, was a fresh graduate and had joined a couple of months before me.

Then there was this girl named Shazia, who was in her mid-thirties and liked to dress very fashionably. Lastly, the marketing head was Mr. Shahzad. Later, Ms. Ayesha told me that the aged man who had interviewed me was Mr. Asghar Malik, and the younger one was the Boss's partner, a certain Mr. Taimur. The first two weeks were counted as my training time, then I was told about the various jobs that I had to do. I was supposed to do inward and outbound correspondence, liaise within the company, and coordinate with sister companies. Then an additional task was assigned to me, Customer Relationship Management! To be honest, my plate was full. I would arrive a little before 9 am, which was the actual office timing, and leave after 5 pm, exactly at the office closing hours. The staff was generally helpful, and I got along well, except that there existed an eerie feeling when people spoke about Mr. Ashgar Malik or were asked to see him in his small office. He was a strange kind of man, there were times when he would mingle with the staff, and then there were times when he would act stone cold, in fact, like a rock. Luckily, I rarely saw him. He was mostly either away on business or confined to his small office.

After three months into my job, I started feeling at home. The environment was fine, the place comfortable, and it was easy getting around with the people. But still, there existed an ill feeling regarding Mr. Asghar Malik. When people spoke about him, it was mostly in hushed tones, or they preferred not to speak in front of everyone. I am not much into gossip and rumors, but several times, I overheard the ladies discussing something about him in covert words. Even then, I just ignored it. Then one day, Waseem did not come to work; Ms. Ayesha informed me that he was unwell and that I had to fill in his place. It meant more work for me that day. I got engrossed in work from morning till evening, skipped lunch instead, and had a few cookies and coffee. It was around 5.30 pm, which, according to my schedule, was quite late, and I was packing up when I heard Shazia speaking to someone on the phone, and a little while later, she started weeping. At first, I thought of ignoring it, considering it to be her problem, but then the good Samaritan in me woke up, and I went to her cubicle and asked if everything was fine. She just wiped her tears and said nothing, tried to smile, and, after some time, left the office.

The next day, when I spoke of last day's incident to Ms. Ayesha, she told me to ignore it and that perhaps Shazia had some personal problems which needed looking after. She also chided me for snooping in on her and, in a way, rebuked me. I was taken aback; I was trying to be helpful and supportive, yet there was this lady who wanted to scold me for doing so. I even contemplated speaking to the HR Department, but when I learned that Mr. Asghar handled the HR matters, I changed my mind. Two days later, the new month started, but I did not get my salary this time. I was surprised since it had never happened before, so I asked Ms. Ayesha, who said she would check it with the finance people. Anyways, I got busy with work and around midday, Ms. Ayesha asked me to speak to Mr. Asghar Malik regarding my salary as there was some issue.

You know, when she told me to speak to Mr. Asghar, I got that weird feeling that, deep down, she knew something was wrong. I mean, for once, she did not look me in the eyes when she suggested I go to Mr. Asghar's office. I went to his office and knocked lightly on the door; on the third knock, I heard him say, "ajao". As I walked into his office, that being my first time, I found it dark and devoid of extra lights, save for a table lamp on his table and some light filtering in through the dark window blinds. He looked at me for an eternity and merely said, "baitho". I told him, "sir I wanted to speak to you about a problem". He replied, "everyone has problems, so what is your problem?" When I told him I hadn't received the previous month's salary, he lit a cigarette, blew out the smoke, and again looked me in the eye for what seemed like eons. After a considerable good time, he asked, "chai peeyo gi?" I shifted uncomfortably in my chair; I mean, here is this man, and here I am asking him about my salary, and instead, he's asking me about tea! What the heck? I politely declined his offer, saying that I had a lot of work to do that day. Instead, Mr. Asghar gave me a hard stare and, almost half smiling, said, *"aj tumhara kaam Shahzad ker lega."* I started feeling more awkward with each passing minute. He kept staring at me for a while, and then he got up and approached me. I had that feeling something very bad was going to happen. On instinct, I stood up and backed up; in fact, I wanted to leave that room immediately. But he sped past me and stood in my way. And then, for what seemed like an eternity, he leered at my body as if undressing me with his eyes. It was the first time I felt exploited, and frankly, I was scared. The man had this quality: he could make anyone uncomfortable with his looks. Mr. Asghar took out his wallet and held it out to me, saying, *"iss mein jitne paise hain le lo, salary ajaye tu wapis ker dena."* At That particular moment, I took his wallet and threw it towards his table. As his attention diverted, I dashed out of the room, went straight to the restroom and tried to compose myself; I was trembling. And then I lost composure and started weeping. It took me a long time to regain my senses. Next, I went to my office, got my belongings and went home.

My mother sensed something was wrong, so she inquired about it, and I satisfied her by saying I wasn't feeling well. I went to my room and lay on my bed, thinking about the day's happenings. I contemplated whether to report about Mr. Asghar or not. But then, whom would I report to? He was the HR, besides so many things in that small office. The more I thought about it, the more I got worried. I feared not getting paid or, worse still, losing my job. Since getting the job, things have become a little easier for our family. But what if I lost it?

The next day, I spoke to Ms. Ayesha about it, and she scolded me for being rude to Mr. Asghar. In her opinion, he had been kind and polite to me. His intentions were good, so he courteously asked me for tea and even offered financial help by loaning me some money. I was bewildered. I did not know what to do. From that day onwards, I immersed myself in office work and never spoke to anyone except for work-related things. A week later, I got my salary. It was such a relief to get my salary. But the relief was short-lived. The month passed peacefully, but again, the next month, I did not get my salary. This time, I decided to wait it out. Two weeks went by, and I still did not get paid. Frustrated and helpless, I again spoke to Ms. Ayesha, and as usual, she assured me to sort it out. An hour later, she returned and asked me to see Mr. Asghar regarding my salary! "Oh, God! No way, I thought, not again." But then, what else could I do? Once again, I went to his office and knocked on his door; after three knocks, I heard him say, *"ajao Jani."* It was as if he knew I was on the other side of the door, and he took immense pleasure in teasing me. Slowly, I walked into his office; he motioned me to sit and said half smilingly, *"Tum phir agai?"* I told him I hadn't got my salary again. The man shamelessly smiled and said, *"Bohat buray log hain yeh finance walay, chai peeo gi?"* Being a nincompoop as ever, I let my guard down and said, *"Ji"*.

The man smiled and ordered two cups of tea. When the tea boy came in and served us tea, Mr. Asghar told him to leave. He picked up a cup of tea and asked me how much sugar I liked. I told him, "One, please" he instantly replied, *"Pehle hi itne meethi ho "* and handed over the cup to me. We had tea in silence while he undressed me with his looks. Finally, he spoke up and said, "let's have dinner together someday". I almost dropped my cup at which he laughed a little and said, *"uff Allah."* I badly wanted to throw the cup on his face, but I feared losing my job. Then mustering up some courage, I said, "sir I need my salary, my family needs it." He looked at me and smilingly picked up the intercom, called the finance manager and told him to sort out my salary issues. That done, I politely thanked him and came out of his office. When I came home, I got an SMS from the bank informing me that my salary had been credited. I thanked God and went to sleep.

The next day, Ms. Ayesha came to me and asked if my salary had been credited. I told her the whole story, to which she said, "you really need to thank Mr. Asghar, for helping you out. He is such a nice person." Not convinced, I asked Shazia what to do. She said absent-mindedly, *"tumhari marzi hai."* At tea time, one of the girls, Tooba, came over to me and whispered in my ear, "salary issues resolved?" I was surprised; how could she know about it? When I told her that my salary had been credited, she said meaningfully, "why don't you go out and have dinner with sir Asghar, he is such a nice man, he will take care of you." I was now beside myself. It doesn't take a superior level of IQ to understand that this message was from none other than Mr. Asghar. This time, I decided to speak to Ms. Ayesha about it. After listening to me patiently, she plainly said, "why are you overreacting? Mr. Asghar might have joked about it while I know Tooba, she's a spoiled child."

And with that, I went to my office and got busy with work.

I distinctly remember that December morning, we had lots of work to do, reports to make, handling paperwork and whatnot. And to make matters worse, Shahzad hadn't come to the office that day, and again, I had to fill in his place. Shazia asked me to make a few photocopies which I, in any case, dreaded, but with an unwilling heart, I took the stack of papers and went into the copying room, "the smallest place on earth," as I used to call it. While making copies, a few sheets fell on the floor, and I bent down to pick them up. Suddenly, the lights went out, and someone grabbed me from behind in a tight grip. His groin touched my buttocks while his hands groped me in the dark, and I heard Mr. Asghar saying, *"dinner pey chalo na jaani, ya phir tumhari salary band kerni paregi?"*. Then just as suddenly as he had appeared, he left and was gone. I fell on the floor, shivering and weeping. A while later, power was restored, and I, looking disheveled and shaken, went to see Ms. Ayesha. When I told her what had happened to me, she asked me to wait in my office and went away. Just then, Shazia, sitting nearby and having heard everything, gave me a glass of water and told me to relax. She empathetically put her hand on my shoulder and said, "you're not alone". I couldn't understand her and was perplexed whether this remark was to console me, give me strength or tell me that she and the other girls in that dreaded company were undergoing the same torture. A few minutes later, Ms. Ayesha came and told me that the Boss was calling me in his office. I followed her to the Boss's office; in his office, I found him sitting on his huge revolving chair, along with his partner Mr. Taimur and Mr. Asghar sitting around his table. When I entered his room with Ms. Ayesha, they stopped talking and told us to sit down. Then the Boss, Imran Kareem, spoke to me and asked me if I had anything to report. I narrated the whole ordeal to him from the very first instance to the last. He asked Mr. Asghar, "lala what's this?" Mr. Asghar smiled and refuted all the allegations as baseless and concocted stories. He, however, mentioned that he had offered tea to me only once on my first visit to his office, which I had declined and that on the second visit, I had asked for tea in a "rather friendly manner".

And regarding the event in the photocopy room, it was baseless and a fabrication to malign him. Just then, the Finance Manager was called and asked to explain why I had yet to get my salary on time, not once but twice. He said it was some issue with the bank since I had not done my biometric authentication in time, which was partly true. Tooba was called too, who flatly denied ever extending an invitation to me for dinner on Mr. Asghar's behalf. And then, the Boss's partner called in the IT guys and asked them to get the latest CCTV footage of the area around and in the photocopy room. The wait lasted for half an hour, and the IT guys, as expected, returned empty-handed, saying there was no CCTV footage because of the power failure and that Mr. Asghar had never left his office. There was no evidence to prove my allegations, and this all was somehow smartly managed by them in the most cunning way. Addressing me, Boss Imran Kareem said that this was the first time he had heard anything against Mr. Asghar and that he had been an efficient employee who was honest and very valuable for the organization. At that moment, I felt like pulling my hair out, yelling at all of them and perhaps killing at least one. All this time, Asghar had that weird smile on his face, which expressed, "see I won, and you lost." The Boss told me that I had been given employment at the behest of some high-ranking office and that I wasn't competent enough to get employment like this anywhere. He then asked me to apologize to Mr. Asghar, to which I flatly refused. As a result, my termination orders were issued verbally there and then, and I was fired from the job just like that. With teary eyes, I packed my stuff while Ms. Ayesha gave me my termination orders. As I left she held me by the hand and whispered, "You should have accepted the dinner invitation."

JATTA

GC Number 165243, Tahir Jameel, aka *Jatta*, as his coursemates called him, was on restrictions for that week. It was summer; the GC was in the third term, or *Uppers* as they were called. Being on restrictions in the prestigious Pakistan Military Academy meant you won't be able to go on short leave or vacations, won't be able to watch the movies, won't be allowed to visit the cafeteria; precisely, it meant a Gentleman Cadet or GC as they were called, was grounded. In simple terms, it meant no recreation; without recreation, life in PMA is hell. Therefore, Jatta was going through hell that week. But frankly, Jatta has been accustomed to it since he landed in PMA a little over a year ago. GC Number 165243, Tahir Jameel, aka Jatta, was known for his quick quips, good looks and physical fitness, good in academics, good in sports and for being the worst in the discipline. The 5 '10" boy from Jhelum was blessed with a slim but strong body, an able mind, and above all, a lion's heart but an offset of a troubled childhood due to which he had spent most of his time in the street fights and brawls, chasing young college girls and hence even lesser time in studies.

When the weekend arrived, Jatta became more impatient; the restrictions meant he would have to attend a fall-in parade each time a Bugle was called, which happened after every 60 minutes, without fail. The Duty Staff would call out the names of all those present, check their names in the register, confirm their presence and then let them go. But on that particular Sunday, Jatta had to go to the city on out pass. He had to meet his newest love Madiha, a beautiful doctor-to-be student of Ayub Medical College, studying in 4th year. She had lost her heart to his disarming looks in a bookshop in Saddar, Abbottabad, while looking for a medical book. Likewise, Jatta had found her to be stunning, cute and loveable and was there to buy *Norwegian Wood,* a book by Haruki Murakami, to be exact. The gutsy officer-to-be had walked up to her and asked for her cell number after having introduced himself merely as Tahir. She had found him attractive and polite but had fallen for his guts. And so that particular Sunday in July, Jatta changed into civil clothes and, making use of one of the smaller holes in the barbed wire fence, sneaked out of the PMA, walked some distance, ran a little, hailed a taxi and went straight to Abbottabad Saddar to meet his love, Madiha at the appointed place and time.

Those few loveliest hours of holding hands, mesmerizing glances and a kiss had felt like Heaven. Hence in a trance, Jatta had missed six roll calls as the incessant Bugle had sounded each time without fail, and his name had been called. He was marked missing from every parade, which in the PMA lingo was unheard of and a Major Sin akin to Gunah e Kabira in Islam. But can you reason with a man in love or, for that matter, a woman? While one is in the company of their beloved stealing kisses, aren't stolen kisses the best?

The following day, he was marched into the Platoon Commander's office on a charge of missing the parade six times; who had found Jatta's reason for absence to be absurd and had referred him to the Company Commander, who, after much fuming and foaming had referred the matter to the Battalion Commander, a certain Lt Col from the Armored Corps, known to eat GCs alive! As the Bugle was heard that particular Monday, GC Number 165243 Tahir Jameel, aka *Jatta*, was marched into the Battalion Commander's office; his platoon mates and course mates had waited with certain hopelessness of the outcome, as it was known that Jatta would either be relegated or withdrawn from the Academy, such was the nature of his offense. Well, the Batallion Commander, after having asked him his cogent reason for absence and after having listened to his love story, had given just a speck of a smile and told him to "Fuck off" from his office.

The handsome Lt Col from Armored Corps valued people who did not lie, were truthful and honest, and that only became the reason for Jatta's respite. The Lt Col remembered his old days at the Academy and, in those few seconds, reminisced about his fling with a certain young teacher from one of the leading schools in Abbottabad, Burn Hall, to be exact. Had lit a cigarette and had gone into a certain inexplicable state of stupor for a few minutes. When Jatta returned to the Barracks, everyone asked him about the matter, to which he had told them the truth, and the whole Academy had called him a lucky bastard! For that is exactly what he was, reckless, brave and truthful.

When his Platoon Commander had called him for a debrief about his meeting with the Battalion Commander, he had chided Jatta for his irresponsible behavior. In the company of his colleagues, the other Platoon Commanders he had later remarked, "This bastard will not make it past a Captain's rank!". But that's how Jatta was, who had led the "mile" throughout his two years at PMA, had never failed a single physical fitness test, set a PMA record for Assault Course, was an excellent shot, had always been amongst the top runners in 5 miles, had been good in studies, confident with all the soldierly and leadership qualities, a great sportsman but also one of the most ill-disciplined GC's in the Academy's history. He had a mad following of lovers and a few haters in cadets and officer cadre. But that was him, Jatta, the ever-confident and favorite of most of them.

Had it not been for his lax discipline, he might have been an appointment holder and a strong contender for the much coveted Sword of Honor. But then, he would not have been Jatta; he would have been anyone else. Like an untamed horse, he enjoyed the frequent trysts with the system, challenging the status quo and always being the odd one out, the eccentric one, instead of being the conformist, as was the norm and requirement in the military. His strong points were his bravado, courage, confidence, honesty, truthfulness, physical fitness, and soldierly qualities. The weak point was his pride, perhaps and his inability to accept run-of-the-mill orders given to him. He would, for example, be late for sports in the evening and physical training sessions in the morning but come to the monthly and quarterly physical efficiency tests, and none in the whole Academy, soldier, cadet or officer could match him. He had knocked out every one of his opponents in the boxing ring.

Despite his shortcomings in discipline, he made it to the final term and passed out in the top bracket as a Second Lieutenant, setting a few academic and physical fitness records and finally got posted to an Infantry Battalion. The delinquent officer joined his unit somewhere in interior Sindh and started his military career on a high note. Jatta soon became the favorite in the unit due to his qualities. All field tasks were given to him, and he performed them to the best of his abilities and thus gained the admiration of his seniors. Here, he befriended his immediate senior, a subaltern from the frontier region, a certain Gul Muhammad. Gul was his immediate senior, a mere six months' seniority meant that they would undergo most of their courses together, train together, run together, laugh together, cry together and perhaps even die together.

Gul was a big-hearted man, just like Jatta, he was brave and selfless, but Gul wasn't ill-disciplined. In fact, he was the perfect example of a disciplined soldier. Jatta told everything about the blue-eyed love of his life Madiha to Gul. They had met and fallen in love instantly, and now she was almost a doctor, and they intended to marry. Madiha and Jatta stayed in touch through letters and phone calls, but somehow he preferred letters over phone calls as he was a little old school in some ways. There was something very romantic about receiving a letter. You could pour your heart out to your beloved on a piece of paper. It could be any length, there were no rules, it was cheap, and hell, yes, it was very romantic. They made plans to get married as soon as Madiha's house job was over. Jatta would dream about the days; he would mostly plan on how to live life with Madiha. It's the best feeling in the world when you're in love. When you're in love, everything looks beautiful; problems don't seem to be problems, there is always hope, and there is always the will to live; it is like living in Heaven. When you're in love, you are afraid and brave at the same time. When you're in love, the world looks perfect!

Then came the day when Jatta received posting orders for Siachen, the highest battlefield. It was to be a six months stint, mandatory and was known to be a tough assignment. Living in sub-zero temperatures with minimum supplies was one thing, and fighting a war in those deplorable conditions was another. So, the young Captain with barely three years' service and three pips on his shoulders reported to his new duty station, Siachen. Subalterns are known to be the most carefree people in the world, they have very few needs, and for them, each day is full of fun. Jatta was assigned a lonesome post well above 21,000 feet, with a crew of ten soldiers and automatic weapons. It was so desolate that people had jokingly named it the "Lost Post". There were few means of communication with the outside world except for a walkie-talkie, mostly used for receiving orders from the HQ, and a commercial radio that gave them much-needed news about the happenings in the world.

Of course, people did get letters once a fortnight, provided someone back home wrote to them. Jatta kept in touch with Madiha through letters. It was her letters that kept him alive and hopeful. He would read her letters when he was down, read them first thing in the morning, and read them before going to bed. And he always kept them inside his Parka, close to his heart. Just about after two months, the letters from Madiha became infrequent. After another month they stopped arriving. The last one mentioned some issues at home. Using the telephone at such a place was out of the question, as communications were non-existent at far-off places. So all he could do was write to her. And he wrote almost daily to Madiha. Another two months and letters that he had written to her were returned to Jatta, unopened and unread…

In mid-June, his stint at Siachen ended, and he was posted back to his unit. But all he could think about was Madiha. On his way back, he went to Madiha's College in Abbottabad and got the sad news that she had been married off to a distant cousin of hers! Jatta could not believe it at first. But then he, despite the wishes of his heart, he went to see her one last time. There she was, just as beautiful as ever, working in a ward, with the doctor's white coat on and a stethoscope around her neck. When she saw Jatta, she just froze, a look of utter disbelief in her eyes, for there in front of her was her beloved, Jatta.

They did not talk much at the Cafe as she sat in front of him trying to sip tea, and even he was indecisive about what to say or what not to say to her. Finally, he got the courage to ask her, and with tears in her eyes, Madiha told him she got married against her wishes, on the insistence of her dying father. Heartbroken, Jatta walked out of the Cafe with his world broken into a million pieces. After that, Jatta wasn't the same Jatta that he had been. When he reported back to his unit and told Gul about it, Gul was understanding and sympathetic but told him something about fate. For Gul, in the past six months, had been proselytized after joining the Tableeghi Jamaat. He had grown a beard and had become deeply religious in his beliefs. In fact, he gave a few sermons to Jatta, which did not have any effect on Jatta, for something in him had died. And to make up for it, he started drinking, a little at first and then a lot.

The weeks were long and busy but come weekends; things would take a slow pace; the dinner nights, Tombola sessions at the Club, the sports galas, movies and billiards matches were the officer's favorite pastimes. And as was wont to happen, a few damsels threw their hearts out to him as he was a good-looking man, something which the women found irresistible. The young subaltern was a favorite heartthrob in the garrison town. It was those times when the country was caught in a wave of terrorism, and his unit had to move to the Northern part of the country to quell the wave of uprising by foreign-supported elements. With a heavy heart and many regrets but also with an imbued spirit of patriotism, they bid farewell to the garrison. They moved to the new location amid promises of return…

It was in Swat that the unit was tasked to clear the strongholds of terrorists. All the towns had been cleared, and people had been forced out of their homes. Camps had been established for the internally displaced persons, or IDPs as they were called. The public was in a quandary; they didn't want to side with the terrorists but had no choice. The Government wanted to free them but was quite helpless as most of the areas were controlled by terrorists. Girls' schools had been destroyed, police stations were being used by the terrorists as torture cells to control the entire region, hospitals were dysfunctional, music had been banned, barber shops closed, and artists had mostly ran away to escape the wrath of terrorists. Life was at a standstill; the public was scared, as people were flogged in public, some killed and hung in the chowks, while the weak preferred to look away. Those who could, did run away. There were no informants for the Army; in fact, the people had been forced to spy on the Army. This was a totally new environment for the Army, and the units were in deep despair. The Commanding Officer would call a meeting of the officers daily to get a brief about the previous day's events and to listen to the next day's plan.

Luckily, Gul and Jatta landed in the same company; they shared a tent that served as their living quarters, dined in the same officers' mess, went for missions together and were almost always together. Jatta threw himself wholeheartedly into the job and would plan each mission down to the smallest detail himself. His hard work paid off as he accomplished the tasks assigned to him in the best possible manner. And slowly, he gained confidence while his Commanding Officer came to trust him more and more. Hence all the difficult missions in the terrorist-infested areas, which also happened to be their area of responsibility, were in one way or the other assigned to their unit and landed in Jatta's lap. The man was known never to say NO; he was a lion-hearted soldier, not scared of anything, not in the least from a few thousand foreign-trained terrorists.

Toward the start of September, orders for a full-scale assault came from the Army HQ, which meant a full-scale operation would be launched, with all soldiers and officers on board to clear the valleys of the scourge that had infested their motherland. As expected, Jatta's unit was to spearhead the operation and to do that, they had to capture a very dominating height, the stronghold of terrorists, one which provided a clear view of the whole valley and gave an uninhibited view to the holder. Undoubtedly, Jatta was chosen to lead the assault. The success or failure of the mission would decide the fate of the whole operation. Everything hinged now on the first operation, being led by Jatta. And so Jatta got down to detailed planning for the mission; he read the maps, reconnoitered the area, flew a reconnaissance mission on a helicopter, got intel through various informants and finally had a plan ready for implementation. A week later, the final go-ahead was given. At first light, on a clear day, Jatta, after having assembled his men and after having given them a pep talk, raised the slogans of *Allah o Akbar* and *Pakistan Zindabad*, and marched on to his objective.

The Commanding Officer had been monitoring the operation from his Command post; it had been progressing slowly; his unit, being led by Jatta, had been making steady progress, gaining ground every minute; the casualties on both sides had been reported as "*heavy*". Both sides were adamant and held on to their positions, for each side knew what failure meant for them. For the terrorists, it would be a total rout; for the Army, a defeat; none was ready to lose it. By midday, his unit had reported reaching halfway to the objective after experiencing heavy fire from automatic weapons and losing many precious lives. Another hour and things began to cool down, fatigue took in, and morale dropped. It was then that the CO personally spoke to Jatta and ordered him to take charge of the situation. Jatta now took personal command of the pilot platoon and resumed the operation with full vigor, with a resolve to take the high mountain, the enemy's stronghold. The fight resumed and became more bloody; as Jatta saw a few heavy weapons firing directly at his men, he called for assistance and requested air support. Two gunships appeared within minutes and flushed out the enemy's positions. Now nothing stood in the way; Jatta and his platoon rushed to get to the top, a well-planned *Charge* that was supposed to turn the tide in their favor.

A little before sundown, the CO received news of the high mountain being captured by his men and the total annihilation of the stronghold. The very few who survived were either taken prisoners or ran away. The news was reported to Brigade and Divisional HQs, amidst great joy and jubilation. And right after that, the radio operator reported Captain Tahir Jameel, aka Jatta, was badly wounded by direct fire from an automatic weapon. An air ambulance was called to evacuate him, but that being almost sundown with limited visibility, could not materialize. And so, by the time the stretcher-bearers transported him to the medical station, Jatta had embraced martyrdom. He had been declared a Shaheed. He was no longer alive. He had given the ultimate sacrifice and, in doing that, had upheld the name of his unit and paved the way for the Divisional assault.

Two months after that, the whole valley stood clear; everyone knew it was due to the heroic action of Jatta that the valley now stood clear. Jatta was laid to rest with full military honors, and with him died his love for Madiha, as he was committed to earth. The darling of the unit was dead. Madiha read of his heroic action and his death in the newspapers, she was obviously heartbroken, but it was too late then. Too late! Jatta was posthumously awarded the Tamgha i Basalat for his services to the nation. True to his Platoon Commander's words, "he did not make past a Captain's rank"! But that was Jatta!

JE T'AIME

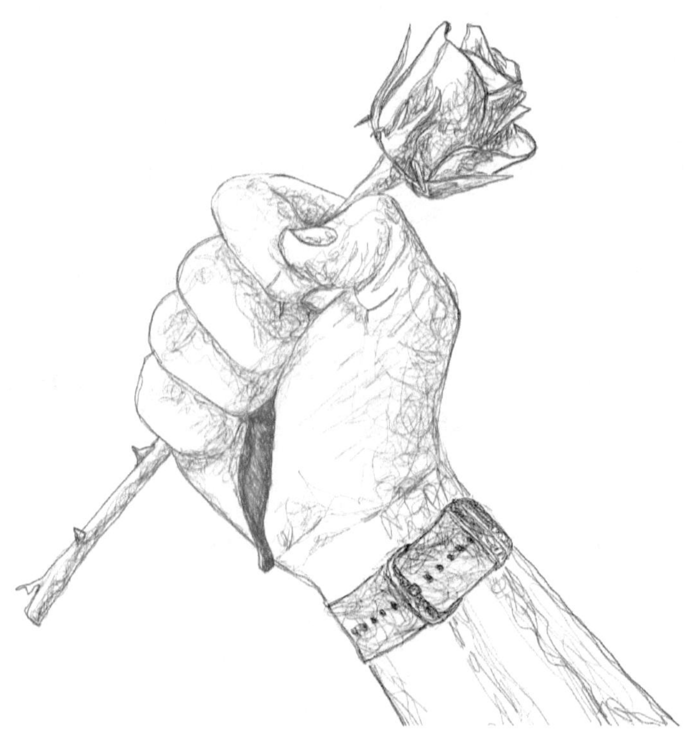

That beautiful mid-May morning, when Shehla Abrar walked into the University of Azad Jammu and Kashmir Muzaffarabad campus to attend the inaugural session of BS Allied Health Sciences, she felt a certain pride in herself. Pride because she, the daughter of a lower-grade employee of the Public Works Department AJK, a Lower

Division Clerk to be exact, had lived a hard life. Out of all her siblings, she was the youngest and also of the least priority for her father as far as education was concerned. Lowest because she would ultimately be married off and would be more suited for house chores. So with meager finances, it was thought that spending money on her education would be a waste of time. During her primary education, Shehla had shown exceptional results at the local Government school in Bagh, AJK and had won a scholarship. She was determined to pursue education despite all the odds. Being a top student, she had won a scholarship to the University. Shehla had chosen Allied Health Sciences as her main program because she wanted to serve her community in a better way after her graduation. And so, with limited resources, strong will and high hopes, she had joined her University that beautiful mid-May morning.

On the same day, Tabish Kareem also walked into the same University for the inaugural session of his BS Electrical Engineering program. He, the son of a local Government officer, had had an easier life. He had mostly lived in Muzaffarabad and had been educated in better schools, all English medium. The only son of his father, Tabish, was a little bit spoiled from the beginning but was known to be kind-hearted to everyone. He loved Cricket, liked to read books, watch movies and listen to Pakistani music; Coke Studio was his favorite regardless of the singers. For all obvious reasons, he started smoking in matric. The fair-skinned, medium-height Tabish with a thick crop of jet-black hair and mischievous smile was known to be a carefree and happy-go-lucky kid since childhood. On that beautiful mid-May morning, he parked his black Yamaha YBR125 in the shed and started walking towards the Main Hall. He was, in fact, late by a good 15 minutes, but then the carefree son of a Government officer was wont to be late; he was rarely, if ever, in time for anything, anywhere.

The inaugural session turned out to be humdrum as the faculty mostly told the DO's and DON'Ts to the students at the University. There was nothing much to say other than not to smoke on campus, not to mix with the opposite gender, to adhere to timings, to study, to obey rules, to get good grades, to say prayers, to stay away from politics, not to wear jeans and tight fitting clothes (especially for girls), not to play loud music, to stay away from social media, not to get involved in brawls etc. etc. Exactly what all the students always wanted to do, was prohibited or discouraged. And understandably, during those three-plus hours, there was little to do except listening to more boring and irksome talk. However, there were few students like

Shehla, who had come from villages or small cities and were easily overawed by the city kids, their dress and smartphones and the ambiance of the University. The event's highlight was a short refreshment break, where hot samosas, tea and cream-puffed pastries were served.

As Tabish went near the table to get some samosas and tea for himself, he noticed a confused girl standing not very far away from the table, yet eyeing the stuff. She had a fair complexion and jet-black hair; it was the blackest black he had ever seen; the face was a perfect oval with thin arched eyebrows that reminded him of a bow he had once seen in a movie. She wasn't tall nor short; she had a very balanced body that reminded him of a song he had recently heard but could not recall the lyrics nor the singer. And she had blue almond-shaped eyes. While Tabish helped himself to a samosa, he looked at her, smiled and said, *"Free hain, khaa lein, paise nahi lain gey university waley."* Baffled to hear from a stranger, the pretty girl just smiled at him. Only then did he notice that she had two tiny yet visible dimples on her cheeks that appeared when she smiled. Tabish almost fell into those small beautiful love craters. Then followed some chit-chat between the two, during which Tabish came to know that Shehla was from Bagh district, and she came to know that he was from Muzaffarabad. He had enrolled in BS Electrical Engineering, and she in BS

Health Sciences. The quick chat lasted only long enough before they were called for another boring preachy session followed by a registration process that ended much after late afternoon. But the memory of the blue-eyed girl with dimpled cheeks remained fresh in his mind forever....and that had been twenty-four months ago...

Months later, Tabish and Shehla were madly in love, and their falling in love was no less than a miracle. After much effort and through some contacts, he got Shehla's cell number. Later, he found out that she used a plain old keypad-type phone, not a smartphone, since she could not afford a pricey cell phone and instead used the simplest one. Though, Shehla, too, got hold of his cell number through some friends but she needed more courage to call him. One day, her phone rang while she was reading a boring book in her hostel room. She was surprised to see that it was from Tabish. But she preferred to ignore his call that day. However, Tabish was not one to give up easily; he called her every day for the next two and half months, seventy-five days to be exact, at the same time, 5 pm, persistently. Shehla, cognizant of the fact that Tabish was calling her, had not answered the phone even once. The phone calls became a regular thing.

Meanwhile, they would see each other at the University, exchange glances, and smile at each other but would hardly speak a word. Tabish often wondered if Shehla knew that he called her daily. Likewise, Shehla also wondered if Tabish knew that she knew that he had been calling her for almost two and a half months nonstop. And that she had been intentionally ignoring his calls. Then came the seventy-sixth day when he could not call her because he had fallen sick and was running a fever. That day, Shehla waited for his call from 5 pm to 9 pm until she couldn't resist; she picked up her phone and called him. He had answered her call on the third ring, and without saying a Hello, Hi or Assalam Alaikum, she blurted: "aaj phone kyun nahi kiya tum ne?" Knowing that she was aware of the fact all along the past seventy-five days about him calling her every day at 5 pm almost made him weep. All he could say was, "I love you," to which she had reciprocated with the same words. In France, people say "je t'aime" to express love to each other, and that's exactly what Shehla and Tabish chose for themselves. They found it unique and, at the same time, safe to say it even when they were around people in the University. And that had been twenty months ago.....

And then the love brewed with their endless chats almost every night and day, during recess periods and in breaks and during lunch hours and before breakfast and after dinner and almost always. They met at the library and in the dining hall, in the football ground, at Nalochi and Pir Chinasi, and Lower Chattar and Upper Chattar, in the bazaar, at PC Muzaffarabad, in the morning and evening, and at odd hours. Madly in love, they had met almost daily and held hands often but had rarely hugged or kissed each other because that wasn't possible unless they were all alone, which was never possible. And so they kept on loving each other covertly and rarely overtly because it wasn't possible to express love in the conservative society they were born and living in. And so as was wont to happen, the word had spread amongst the students and from them to the teachers and faculty and after that to the rest of the city and the government offices and bazaars, that Tabish, the son of a high-ranking Government officer, renowned in the city was having an affair with a village girl. But with a twist, for it was rumored that the girl had lose character and soon was labeled as *badchalan.* When the news reached the love birds, they cared less for what the people around them said and were more interested in each other. The problem started when the University administration got wind of the matter and called both of them at separate hours to explain their lewd behavior, first verbally and then in writing, and these two poor souls having no sense of things, had said that they were just friends. But the administration decided to get tough on them since the friendship between a boy and a girl was simply unacceptable, so they decided to rusticate both of them for two weeks and allow them to improve their behavior. As a result, Tabish and Shehla had to leave the University for two weeks. During those two weeks, both of them realized the intensity of their love because they could speak to each other on the phone but could not meet or see one another, which was very painful for both of them. Tabish's father stormed at him for such careless behavior and asked him to focus on his studies instead of wasting his time on some village girl, to which Tabish had remained unmoved and had scoffed.

News spread like wildfire and finally reached the small town of Bagh and to Shehla's father about his daughter's rustication. He, a poor but honorable man, found it difficult to face the men of his family who had come to meet him at odd hours inquiring about his daughter despite knowing the truth of the matter well. Overwhelmed with pain and dishonor caused by his daughter, Shehla's father beat her up badly, forbade her to go to University ever again and instead decided to get her married to a distant cousin of hers, who was uneducated and worked as a conductor in a bus company. Being a headstrong girl, Shehla refused the marriage proposal, and just before the expiry of the mandatory two weeks period, one day, she ran away with

Tabish in a car to Muzaffarabad and stayed at a guest house till she joined the University. When her father and relatives came to take her away, she refused to see them and finally shifted to a room rented by Tabish exclusively for her in a desolate part of the city. At last, her father decided to disown her and vowed never to speak to or have any relationship with her. And it was known that he had instructed his sons to kill her, but they had refused to comply…… that had been seventeen months ago….

Life moved on, and then the University organized a study tour to distant locations, and students were offered to be taken to Islamabad and other cities. Both Tabish and Shehla had opted for Islamabad because Islamabad was one city where they could meet openly without inhibitions. With countless dreams and aspirations, they left for Islamabad on the University bus for a four day study tour. And in those four days, they rarely parted from each other and explored all the places from Quaid e Azam University to NUST, NUML , SZABIST, IQRA and AIOU together. They loved the food at Saidpur village, Monal and Highland Club, Islamabad Club, Marriott and PC. Tabish had kept his promise and took her to the best restaurants in the twin cities. They had a good time while dining and visiting different places, he also took her shopping, but she refused to buy anything, for she could think of no reason how she would tell her friends or parents about the expensive clothes that he wanted to buy for her. And so they had settled instead for books at a trendy shop called the Saeed Book Bank. As luck would have it, one day, they got to spend some time alone in each other's company. So, they made tea together and had breakfast sitting next to each other. They talked about all the things they wanted to talk about alone in each other's company without fear of being seen, heard, or judged by the people around them. The young couple kissed and hugged each other. Overwhelmed with love, she asked him to kiss her anywhere he wanted to, and being timid; he had opted to kiss her on the forehead, for he had found it very decent and loving. Persistent on her offer, Shehla encouraged Tabish again, to which he had found the courage to lift her shalwar a tad bit and kiss her calf, for he had found it to be very attractive and had never in his life seen a girl with an exposed calf. Shehla had found it to be very romantic and, at the same time, very sexy. They returned to Muzaffarabad more in love than ever, with many sweet memories. And that had been fifteen months ago....

Unbeknown to them, their moves were being observed by those around them, and watchful eyes had been following them covertly. While they dined at restaurants, walked hand in hand, posed for photographs, laughed, smiled and enjoyed the little moments of freedom together, they were being watched. They were reported upon their return to the university officials. This time, the University administration decided to take strict measures, so they gave them written explanations, called their parents, and made a rumpus loud enough to stir up the world. When the local newspapers and the religious zealots got wind of it, the whole city had nothing else to talk about except Shehla and Tabish. What else could the poor souls do? Both of them decided to give statements about their feelings of affection for each other, which almost caused the University to be shut down for a full three days, as the local clergy declared it utterly un-Islamic, and things got worse for both of them. Tabish's father coaxed him to get admission in a better University in Islamabad or perhaps anywhere in the country or even out of the country. Still, he flatly refused to acquiesce to his demands.

On the other hand, Shehla's father had forcibly, with the help of her brothers and relatives, taken her, well almost kidnapped her, in a rented car to Bagh to tie the knot with her cousin, who she had no feelings for and perhaps disliked. And while all this happened, a well-known religious party's on-campus wing comprising of students had almost forced their decision on the administration to ban the two of them, Tabish and Shehla, as according to them the two had set a bad precedent for all students in the University and that it could not be allowed in any case. Therefore, Tabish and Shehla were terminated from the University and were told to get admission elsewhere. With things going south for them, both contemplated running away together to any place where they could be together forever, but they found no such place or relative or friend who could support them in this endeavor. Shehla even thought of going to some NGO that could help them. Still, sadly she did not know, or perhaps there did not exist one that helped or was willing to help lovers because that always had the least priority for anyone; in a country steeped in corruption, violence and hatred, love had a little place, and hopes were low. And that had been thirteen months ago....

And while all this was happening in the city of Muzaffarabad, one day, Tabish was out with friends for dinner at a local hotel, and when he went to the restroom, someone stole his cell phone, and that alone created a furore in the city once again for his cellphone contained both Shehla and Tabish's photographs together. Most importantly, the photographs from their Islamabad visit were copied and shared over social media and within minutes, they went viral in Muzaffarabad. Later, in a matter of hours, the whole of AJK was sharing their photographs with the choicest of expletives and cuss words added to them. The gossip reached a new level where both were rumored to have been sleeping together and that, at one time, Shehla had gotten pregnant and had had an abortion. While all this was happening, Shehla had been forcibly married to her cousin, Jawad. When the news of the affair reached Bagh and her little village, people shared and showed the couple's photos to everyone and chided them as immoral and *beghairat.* One after the other, things turned ugly for Shehla. Just a few hours after her marriage, she was sent home by her husband, beaten badly, only after being bedded. Despite her chastity, he called her a *Gashti;* deep inside, he knew that even then, he had left her owing to society's hearsay and gossip because it was a matter of honor for him. And that had been a little more than ten months ago…

Apparently, the nightmare had finished for the world, but the lovebirds still had to meet their fate. Both Tabish and Shehla were housebound and had found it hard to meet each other though they were in touch, heartbroken and hopeless. Shehla's father had threatened to kill her, but her brothers intervened, thus saving her life. Because he now found her a stigma on his name and honor. Tabish had brooded hard over his situation and had found no answers anywhere that could give him a plausible solution to his problem. So, he called Shehla on the phone and asked her to pack just the bare essentials before anyone came to know about their plan, and when he came to get her, she jumped into his car and eloped with him to Muzaffarabad. Word got around soon, and Shehla's father and brothers reported the matter to the Police, who sent urgent messages over the wireless to all police stations to be on the lookout for two absconding lovers. Obviously, the whole of AJK, having seen their photos, knew well who they were looking for.

Luckily, Tabish and Shehla had escaped by the time the Police could get them though Tabish was certain that Shehla's father and brothers would chase them down. It was a desperate decision, taken by them in haste, it wasn't logical or rational, but then that is what love is all about. Irrational and illogical. While they were discussing the options, still hopeful, Tabish got a call on his cellphone. Shehla's brother demanded that he hand over Shehla to them, and they would for sure spare his life. Tabish's young mind was not ready to part with Shehla; they had vowed to be together in life and death. Staying together wasn't possible, as was staying away.

At least while they were alive, none could imagine a life without the other. It was always a dead end, with no support or help in sight. Eventually, they decided to pass on to the other side together. While Tabish did not want to end it this way, he had no choice, and while Shehla did not want to continue this way, she had no choice either. They drove to Zulfiqar Ali Bhutto suspension bridge, got off their car hand in hand, looked each other in the eyes, smiled and almost in unison said, "Je t'aime" and jumped off the bridge into the river. A few locals tried to stop them, but it was too late. Their bodies were carried off by the fast currents of the river, visible on the surface for a few yards, and ultimately drowning in the depths of the river.....

A day later, both bodies were recovered from the Kohala bridge, where the river's flow slowed to a crawl. They were spotted by a group of students picnicking in the area, just a few feet apart. Tabish and Shehla had passed on to the other side together; they had been victims of a hypocritical society, one that did not believe in rational thinking, was judgmental, was stagnant with age-old traditions and was not concerned about individuals, had little or no space for love in their hearts and one where love had no value or respect. Both Tabish and Shehla were buried in their native towns, quite unceremoniously, as according to the local Mullahs, they had committed suicide, which was *Haram* and thus did not deserve a funeral. Both Tabish and Shehla now sleep peacefully while the world continues to try to find peace in their hearts. And that had been six months ago….

When two lovers die, their love is given back to the world manifolds; hence the aspiring young hearts looking for love catch just a speck of it to rekindle the fire; thus, the cycle repeats itself, and love flourishes, it never dies!!

KITTY PARTY

Mrs. Khan had had her third cup of coffee, but still, the hangover would not go away. The night had been busy and wild. There were guests, and she had been busy attending to them. By the time she went to bed, it was almost 2 in the morning. She woke up at 8 in the morning to go to a coffee party. Well, it was more than that; her close friend Shehla had arranged for a religious scholar to lecture the guests at the monthly Committee Party. This was a norm in the quiet and peaceful neighborhood of Bilal Colony. The committee parties were a monthly feature, with a religious sermon in between. They were all so happy about it, always. It was Kaar-e-khair, and they wanted to reap the benefits of it. In between, they could eat, talk and enjoy while one of the members was sure to get some money as her committee would mature that month and with all this, they would get a dose of gossip for the month. She took a shower, got ready and went to the party. It was winter, and the Sun was out in the city of Lahore. It was a beautiful day, and they would make the most of it.

By the time Mrs. Khan reached Shehla's house, it was packed with guests. There was Mrs. Baari, the lady with the fat nose; there was Mrs. Aftab, who walked with a stoop, the venerated Mrs. Ansar, who was just perfect save for her husky voice, Mrs. Jaan, who was a fine lady but could not agree to anything that anyone said, to name a few. Orange juice had already been served, and when Mrs. Khan found a place to sit, she had to ask for one. They were all discussing the religious scholar who was there to deliver the sermon. She looked kind of small to Mrs. Khan, who joked about the scholar to all her friends. Most of them agreed and giggled; some gave inward smiles, while one or two preferred to keep to themselves. Shehla had arranged the scholar through a friend of hers. She had told Shehla that the scholar was a very respectable and knowledgeable lady. A lady she held in great reverence, for she was known to be straightforward and, well, a little nosy.

In about fifteen minutes, the lecture started, and all the ladies covered their heads with stoles and focused on the scholar. The scholar was one learned lady, or so it appeared; she began the sermon by criticizing the situation in society and the moral degradation prevalent. She talked about the sins being committed by all, of the gross insubordination to Allah's injunctions, the injustice to the poor, the vulgarity on TV channels, the fashion fever, the music revolution, the insolent children, the irresponsible parents and everything in between. But then this was just the introduction, for she mentioned that the lecture was purely on backbiting that day. She told them of the various sayings of the Prophet (PBUH) condoning this sin; she lectured them against it in the light of the Quran's teachings; she forbade them from it, telling them of the social evils resulting from this sin; she cautioned them against it as it was as bad as eating a dead brother's meat. Silently all nodded and absorbed the deeply penetrating words of the scholar; they looked at each other in between and exchanged smiles; they pondered over it in their hearts and let out sighs of remorse. They felt bad about it; they felt guilty, some whispered to their immediate neighbors in muffled sounds, and they all regretted doing it at one time or the other. They promised themselves in their hearts to resist all such temptations as long as they lived.

Between the lecture, the scholar asked for some water, and Mrs. Alvi quickly brought her a glass. Mrs. Aftab and Mrs. Jaan quickly noted this and exchanged wry looks with each other. Both felt what the other meant to convey with her eyes; they understood those smiles. "A smart move" is what both of them meant to say to the other, alluding to Mrs. Alvi's action. After the glass of water, the sermon resumed with even greater vigor; the lecturer called upon them to give up backbiting, bade them to be real sisters amongst themselves, and asked them to vie against the temptation.

So far, the lecture was going well, and Shehla had sensed it. Shehla stopped the scholar midway and, in a very excited tone, promised her that she would never in her life slander anyone in their absence. At which the scholar praised her, she said prayers in her favor and called the others to follow Shehla's example. She told them that Shehla was on the path to becoming a Momina and that she had the cleanest heart of them all. This time Mrs. Ansar and Mrs. Baari exchanged looks and gave inward smiles to each other. Mrs. Baari had waited a long time for this committee party, for it was her turn to get the money that day. She was getting impatient, for she had planned to go to the market straight from the party. She just did not like Shehla's intrusion into the talk. She knew Shehla very well; she was fashionable and not at all Islamic. Then why this display of piety? She just could not understand. Silently she took out her cell phone and texted Mrs. Ansar the words, "hmm...Momina, my foot. Watch her drama!". A second later, Mrs. Ansar felt her cell phone vibrating in her purse; she took it out and almost laughed at the message. Again the looks were exchanged between the two, this time with more overt smiles.

The scholar told them about hell, heaven and life; hereafter. She told them of the good things awaiting them and the ills of sins; she lectured them to be pious, to be truthful, to be honest, to forgive others and to be good to all. She told them to look deep into their hearts and do some soul-searching. By now, the lecture had been going on for a good one hour, and the ladies were getting impatient. Somehow, the scholar sensed this, and after a while, she ended her sermon with prayers. As soon as the prayers were over, everyone heaved a sigh of relief. They were thankful that it was all over. Some had gained a lot, some little and some none. The mood became somewhat festive. That's when the waiters came in with dishes full of food. There were samosas, dahi bhallay, fruit chat, kebabs, haleem, orange juice, naan, chicken roast, cake, gulab jamuns and whatnot. The ladies helped themselves to huge servings, and everyone started enjoying the food.

Mrs. Ansar, after filling her plate, came to Mrs. Baari and said in a hushed tone, "good arrangement by Momina", at which the latter burst into fits of laughter. Mrs. Baari was somehow not happy because there was no fish on the table, and also that the lecture had been too long. She simply said that it would have been better if the lecture had been shorter and the kebabs a little longer. They laughed again. Soon they were joined by Mrs. Jaan, who joked about Shehla's big mouth and ultra-fashionable clothes. According to her, they did not go with her pious attitude. The trio was joined by Mrs. Khan, who sensing the mood of the group, just could not keep herself away. Mrs. Khan was a jolly woman and was known to be very sweet to everyone. She had friends everywhere, in the colony, in the colony next to them and beyond that. In this circle, she commanded respect from them all. In a definite voice, she addressed them all and said that the religious lecture did not go with the committee party, and it was better they finish it. It wasted a lot of time, and it was better they did some social work in this time instead. Seeing the group of four on to something, it wasn't long before most of the ladies started coming to them. There was Neelum, Asifa, and Ammara, who were neighbors, and Mrs. Amjad, Mrs. Talpur and Sumaira, who lived in the next lane.

Soon enough, everyone was expressing their views on the committee party and that the religious sermon was one thing and the party another. Said Mrs. Talpur, "I really don't like the idea of a sermon, I don't even remember who started it." That's when Sumaira told them it was Shehla's idea initially. "But we are educated women," argued Mrs. Amjad, "we do not need these lectures to teach us." Neelum and Asifa silently nodded while Ammara said, "it is all because of Shehla that we have to bear it. Look at her; she is not the religious type at all, then why this *daras* and sermon?" "We need to finish this", said Mrs. Baari.

Meanwhile, Shehla was attending to the scholar. She made sure that the guest had a little of everything, filling her plate now and then with some Barfi, Samosa, Pakora and chaat. She was happy that the lecture had gone so well. Indeed, all the guests must have gained a lot out of it. She reckoned they must be talking about it too. How right she was.

Finding her plate empty, Mrs. Aftab hastily got up to have another fill. She tried to walk fast, and that's when her stoop became more obvious, which did not go unnoticed by the group of ladies. Asifa was quick to mimic Mrs. Aftab's stoop, and everyone burst into fits of laughter. Ammara quipped, "The hunchback of Notre Dame" that's when Neelum put her finger on her lips, telling her to keep quiet as Mrs. Aftab was returning with a plate full of eateries, who, on returning, asked them about the laughter. Neelum said, "oh we were joking about Shehla's religious views". Mrs. Aftab replied, "well she deserves to be joked about." Now it was Mrs. Ansar who could not hold herself back; she addressed the group in her husky voice, "Shehla is a Momina", again the loud laughter. Everyone seemed to be having a great time. Mrs. Ansar's cell phone rang, and she excused herself to attend the call. Sumaira was quick to cash in on occasion and tried to make her voice sound like Mrs. Ansar said, "Shehla is a Momina,", again the loud and rapturous laughter. They talked about Shehla's fashion, her taste for music, her eating habits, her "drinking habits", her car, her house, her clothes and almost everything about her.

After having food, the room suddenly seemed hot. They switched off the heaters, and someone opened the windows, as it was getting stuffy inside. Mrs. Jaan, after taking a third serving, came to join the laughing ladies huddled in the corner. She sensed someone was missing that day and asked around casually about Mrs. Malik. Mrs. Malik was the third wife of a big businessman, Malik sahib, as he was known. She was in her thirties, well-educated and good-looking. She was known to flaunt her wealth in several ways, like driving the latest model car, wearing the trendiest of clothes, the best of perfumes and frequent makeovers. Asifa, in a very wry way, said, "She must be busy today, shopping for clothes or buying a new car." Neelum felt being left out of this communication quickly joked, "or she might be out getting a makeover." "I really don't care", said Mrs. Jaan. But anyhow, she never misses an event to show off her newest things. Hearing this, Sumaria said, "Who knows, Mailk sahib might be visiting her." At this, they all laughed. "As if he cares' ', said Mrs. Jaan and again, there was more laughter. Mrs. Aftab sensing the moment and looking at Mrs. Jaan, said, "I just don't like the lady; in fact, I hate her." And just then, Mrs. Jaan said, "Although she's lovely and gorgeous in every way, I think she's pretty much hate-able".

After some time, Shehla came towards the ladies huddled together, gossiping and laughing, and seeing her coming towards them, they suddenly went quiet. Shehla, being the lively one, put her arm on Mrs. Jaan's shoulder and asked, "What's this all laughter and gup shup about?". And Mrs. Aftab just piped in, "oh, we were discussing you, actually, what a wonderful party this is and the food is amazing, and really we want to thank you for arranging such a beautiful lecture by a religious scholar". And then Mrs. Baari joined in, and they all started praising her while at the same time eyeing each other and exchanging meaningful looks. And on hearing this, Shehla was actually flattered. She told them it was her idea to introduce the sermon, and she was glad they liked it and found it useful. And just then, Mrs. Baari could not contain herself and asked Shehla, "When do we get the committee?" Shehla took a small basket, as per their custom and held it in front of each of the ladies who took out an envelope each from their wallets and bags and placed them in the basket. While most of the ladies had the money ready in their wallets and some in their bags, it was Mrs. Khan and Bushra only who had it hidden in their secret upper compartment, deep in the confines of aging meat, the safest natural ATM. And the money they pooled in smelt of the best perfumes. After counting the money, she handed over a thick wad of currency notes to Mrs. Baari, who immediately blurted out, "Oh My God, I have an appointment with the doctor." And that, in a way, was a covert signal for everyone present over there that the party had ended and it was time to leave. All the ladies wearing colorful clothes got up, hugged each other as they were sworn sisters and left Shehla's hou--se one by one, none of them being happier than Mrs. Baari.

NOC

91

When Rukhsana Begum's man passed away, she had three kids depending on her. Being a school teacher, she did not have any liabilities as such; she had a house in her husband's name, a small car and some jewelry. Her husband, Meherban Khan, was hardly 48 when he went into God's mercy; thus, Rukhsana was left to bear the burden of her miseries alone. Though Meherban had not left them roofless or destitute but still now she had to shoulder all the responsibilities herself. As is wont to happen in the land of the pure, very few of Meherban's friends, relatives and even Rukhsana's relatives came forward to help her in any way. Not that she had asked for it, rather being a self-willed and strong lady, she had decided to carry on her own. Meherban had a steady job in the Development sector and kept changing jobs as and when opportunities arose. The NGOs paid good money by Pakistani standards, he made a small house, bought a car and had still spare cash for two Educational policies in his kids' names. But when the angel of death came knocking on his door that Wednesday morning on a beautiful September day, the last words he said to his wife while looking into her eyes were, "I love you." And then he was gone, 22 years of association gone in less than a minute. The three orphans cried over it; they yelled and wept like any orphan would. But then, that was the deity's will, for we are all helpless when the time comes for us to depart from this mortal world.

A week after the burial, Rukhsana resumed her duties at school. Her kids were at different stages of life; the eldest had joined University and was studying Electrical Engineering, her daughter was in FSc, and the youngest son was in grade 6. Their world had turned upside down in a matter of minutes. Luckily, Meherban had left them some savings, so they did not have serious financial issues. However, the house was registered in Meherban's name and had to be transferred to Rukhsana's name. This required a lot of legal formalities to be fulfilled; there was the succession certificate which took almost six months from the time of filing till its issuance. She hired a lawyer; he filed a case in the Sessions courts after placing advertisements in the newspapers for legal heirs to come forward and make claims. Thankfully none came, so they waited, and then they waited some more. Sometimes the Judge would be on vacation; at other times, the lawyers would call a strike, and at times her name wouldn't be called by the clerk. It was a test of her nerves, but in about six months' time she finally got the succession certificate, which meant she and her kids were the legal heirs, and she could finally get the house transferred in her name.

The country is being ruled by an elite class, a class that is oblivious to the happenings of the common people. The powerful exude power; they show it as if it is some ornament, something to be proud of. And then, there is a parallel world, an underworld, a huge connected network of clerks, peons, superintendents, assistants, file bearers, watchmen and Naib Qasids. This class has its own privileges and perks; it has its own set of rules, an ethos developed over time, a way of life and a unique culture. While the elite thrive in their own arena, the underworld thrives in its own. Each class has a distinct function, but their paths cross; in fact, they overlap at some places, and the boundaries remain distinct, yet the functions intertwine. Each class needs the other class to survive; they are interdependent, and they cannot work or exist in isolation. Each has defined its rules and boundaries. Deep down, there is seething rivalry between the two, yet on the face of it, they are one. When it comes to safeguarding their interests, each class stands its ground; they hate each other, yet they are forced to smile and acquiesce to the other's wishes. So if you want to get something done from a Government office and you're lucky to know someone or are from the elite class, things will get easier for you. Else you will be forced to take the underworld path.

And so Rukhsana being from a lower class, had no option but to opt for the underworld solution to her problem. To get the house transferred in her name, she had to get the No Objection Certificate, commonly called the NOC. She took a day off from her school and arrived at the Housing Authority offices early in the morning. Sure enough, there was a reception, and the uninterested clerk showed her the way to the transfer office. There was one large window to that office which meant that the public had to interact with the people inside the transfer office through that window. Hanging outside the office was a large banner with the words "One Window Operation" written in bold. The banner had a white background, and the text was in red. In fact, the One Window Operation was actually a window of opportunity for some and a dark abyss for others. It was an opportunity for those who knew someone somewhere and knew how to get things done, by any means necessary, mostly by paying bribes. It was an opportunity for those who knew and understood the system, for those who believed in getting it done anyway, for those who had total disregard for rules or, in the extreme cases, were acquiesced into the ways of the mob, the underworld. And the same window would prove to be an abyss, a dark hole, a bottomless pit for those who did not know anyone, did not believe in bribes and connections, were simple people, believed that things worked how they were projected or told to them. Through the same window, the simple people would come to know that their files had been lost, burnt or, most often, an objection of some absurd nature had been raised by some wicked clerk in an unknown office which, in fact, was the representation of that dark hole that this window actually led to. And in the end, even the simple folk would be forced to take the path of trickery. A system that had evolved over the last 75 years, an impregnable system that did all kinds of dishonesty with all honesty and in a fair manner. That was the rule!

Rukhsana had compiled the list of paperwork required for the transfer; she had seen all the details, not once but many times; she got the papers attested, got the photocopies made, attached the succession certificate and her NIC etc etc. The unimpressed clerk took some time to look through her file and finally stamped it, entered it in his diary and gave her an acknowledgment receipt. The transfer would be done in four weeks, she was told, and so the poor simple lady heaved a sigh of relief and came back home. That day, she did nothing except watch TV and relax.

The promised four weeks passed in a state of anxiety, Rukhsana wanted the house to be transferred in her name as soon as possible, but then procedures had to be followed, and rules dictated a sequence of internal processes, only after which the NOC would be authorized, and the transfer be completed. Exactly after four weeks, she went to the same office with the big window and deftly presented the receipt to the same uninterested clerk, who, after taking a hard long look at the receipt and Rukhsana, rummaged through some old files and went out of the room through a door in the back. As she waited, her heart started beating faster; she prayed for the NOC to be issued and for her agony to end. But that was not to be, as the clerk came back with the sad news that her file was still in processing and would take more time. "More time?" she asked, "how much more time?" He just shrugged and told her to come after two weeks. Thus started an unending sequence of Rukhsana's visits to the same office with the large window, where she would get the same answer. "The file was in processing, and would take more time". She requested the clerk to help her, she wanted to meet the officer responsible for the transfers, but there were none available because the "single window operation" was designed to prevent outsiders from interacting with those responsible; it was necessary, they said, to ensure more transparency and speed. They said it was swift, unbiased and a requirement of modern times. The Chairman of the authority had boasted about the "Single window operation" at many forums, in local print and electronic media. Special laws and rules had been enacted, they said. It was a revolutionary step; it was modernization and a necessity.

As more time passed, Rukhsana became more impatient; only the Succession certificate had taken six months, and now another six months had passed since she had submitted the papers for the transfer of ownership of the house in her name. She tried calling the Helpline of the Housing Authority, but it was useless, and no Help was provided. The website showed the email addresses and phone numbers of the officers concerned with the Department, but she got no reply to her emails, and her calls went unanswered. It was then that her friend's husband suggested she write to the local Parliamentarian of their community to help her. It was said that Mirza Sahib was a God-fearing man who believed in helping anyone who approached him. And so she wrote a long and detailed letter to the MNA sahib, describing her predicament and sought his help.

XXXXXXXXXXXXX

A rather extraordinary meeting of the most powerful people in the country was being held in the Secretariat Committee Room that fine morning. All the big and powerful men and women were arriving one by one. They had artificial plastic smiles on their faces, wore expensive clothes and watches, and arrived in the latest chauffeur-driven cars; the powerful women were dressed up in colorful clothes, they wore the latest perfumes, and the younger ones had makeup on their faces, everything and everyone looked perfect and beautiful. The meeting had been arranged with many important agenda items on the list. They had to decide which types of cars were to be procured for the parliamentarians in the coming year, there was one group who wanted their hostels to be renovated on priority, yet another wanted a substantial raise in their salaries, a small group of people belonging to the opportunistic religious class wanted to go on Umrah at state expense so that they could expiate themselves of the sins they had committed and of course to pray for the country's future. Another group wanted the ban on international travel removed so that larger delegations could go to foreign countries at the state's expense and "study their systems', which they said would be very beneficial for the country. And finally, a small group wanted the Cafeteria bills to be reduced substantially and their traveling and dining allowances revised so that they could serve the public much better. And amongst these groups was one lonely man, Mirza Sahib, who wanted nothing for himself. He was there for the meeting, though. Mirza Sahib was dressed in white Shalwar Kameez and a black waistcoat. He was, after all, a simple person. As usual, the meeting started with greetings by the Chairman to all those who were present and, of course, the customary recitation of the Holy Quran, which was mandatory at all such meetings. The Secretary briefed everyone about the agenda and presented a list of items that were to be discussed. The Chairman, having gone through the agenda items, thanked everyone and congratulated them for selecting such important points for discussion as these were related to the well-being of the parliamentarians. These poor people could only perform better if they were looked after in a better way. They were there to serve the country and its people.

After that, formal discussions started, and one after the other, the agenda items were approved unanimously. After each approval, the group presenting the item would thank and congratulate the others and smile at them, who in turn would feel great happiness deep inside their hearts, for they believed in the democratic processes and wanted the country to progress "at all costs". The lonely stenographer taking down notes belonged to the underworld; he understood each and every point that was being deliberated upon, and deep inside his heart, he loathed their actions and words; he hated them even more, he was helpless, but he knew that the underworld operated differently. They never showed emotions; they smiled and agreed to everything, waited for the right time, and then made the move. In some cases, they had inherited this from their fathers, for in the same country, they had seen a politician's son become a politician, a bureaucrat's son a bureaucrat, a Maulvi's son, a Maulvi and so mostly a clerk's son would be a clerk, and so on. And that is how all of them learned important lessons from their fathers.

Training at home provided them with useful tips on how to go about things, what mistakes to avoid, what to say, and what not to say. As the meeting progressed, plain tea and biscuits were served; the Chairman informed them all that due to the austerity measures, that was all they could be served; after all, Pakistan was a poor country and could not afford such extravagance. One by one, all demands of the public representatives were presented and agreed upon without much deliberation and resistance. It was, after all, their well-being that was being discussed.

Finally, at the end of the meeting, the Chairman thanked everyone and asked if any point was left? There was silence in the room, and then Mirza Sahib rose from his chair, walked up to the Chairman, took a letter out of his pocket, and placed it in front of the Chairman. The Chairman was bewildered; he had this expression of confusion on his face. And on being asked, Mirza Sahib narrated Rukhsana's ordeal to the house. There was a hush in the house. For a long time, no one spoke. Then the Chairman cleared his throat and told the house that he respected Mirza Sahib's feelings and that he admired his courage and will to serve the people of Pakistan. And that No Objection Certificate, in any case, was a requirement for getting any approval from the Government and its related departments. They had made special arrangements, made the processes easy and transparent, and that NOC could not be done away with. Mirza Sahib lamented that the NOC was a great hindrance in most cases. It was used as a tool by incompetent officers for minting money from poor people. It was, in most cases, useless and unnecessary. At this, the house erupted into a heated debate. Each man and woman trying to speak at the same time. They wanted to speak because Mirza had directly threatened them. They knew deep down in their hearts that if the NOC's were done away with, then anyone and everyone could easily get an NOC for almost anything, and this would mean more competition for the people sitting in the house, as each one of them had multiple businesses which they had started after getting the required NOCs by using their influence. The annulment or making the process any easier would mean more competition and hence more loss to their businesses.

A young man from a powerful ruling party remarked that NOC was mandatory, and at the latest count, the various Federal as well as Provincial governments and their departments issued thousands of different kinds of NOCs. And that this kept things in order, without which nothing would work. He even joked that his party was also considering making an NOC mandatory for getting married. At this, the Chairman joked that marriage itself was the biggest NOC, as after that, one could do anything. At this, the house burst into laughter, and the meeting ended with Mirza Sahib losing unanimously. All the poor man had wanted to do was to plead Rukhsana's case to make things easier for the likes of her.

XXXXXXXXXXXXX

When Rukhsana was told through Mirza Sahib's munshi that he could not help her and that the outcome of the meeting and discussions had been unfruitful in her favor, she wept her heart out in front of the munshi. Munshi was an aged man but one with a good heart. He consoled her and said he would help her. It so happened that Munshi's son-in-law worked in the Housing Authority office, and he promised to ask him to help Rukhsana. And he did talk to his son-in-law, so one-morning, Rukhsana arrived at the Housing Authority office and met Munshi's son in Law, Akbar. Munshi and his son in Law were also connected to the undocumented underworld. Akbar listened sympathetically, saw her receipt, dug out her file and told her that he considered her his real sister. He told her he would help her get the NOC and the file approved after speaking to the concerned section in charge. Two days later, she got a call from Akbar asking her to come to the office again; this time, Akbar told her she was lucky that her file was intact even after almost a year. He told her that normally files that aren't approved in such a long time are lost; it was actually a ruse, but poor Rukhsana understood none of this. He also told her that her file had some inconsistency and that it could not be approved; he had personally spoken to the section in charge, who, being a very honest person, had flatly refused to be of any assistance. Later Akbar had, on his own volition, sought help from a tout. The tout, being well connected, would get it done for one hundred thousand rupees. Rukhsana was heartbroken; she was aghast on hearing this, one hundred thousand rupees was a huge sum for her, but she also had to save her house. Akbar also told her that this was a good rate, and if delayed, the charges were sure to increase; however if she paid the required amount, he would waive off the late fees. And so the poor lady sold some of her jewelry and paid the money to Akbar.

Three days later, Rukhsana got a call from the Housing Authority; she was told to come to the "One window operation" office and collect her letter. She went there and got her NOC and transfer letter in a mere 15 minutes.

POSTEE

When the alarm went off at 6 am, I woke up in a blink. I had gone to bed at precisely 10 pm the previous night and had slept for eight hours. Eight hours of sleep was essential for someone like me; I am that perfect example of a self-made man, one who had been born in a poor household, one who had many competing mouths, who had gone to cheap Government schools where they made you sit on the floor, where corporal punishment was still in practice. I had never had any support from anyone. I knew from the beginning I was pretty much on my own. And that was how it had been with me since my early days. I jumped off my bed after drinking the mandatory three glasses of water. I stepped into my small gym and started my strenuous workout consisting of cardio, followed by some power training and finally planks and stretching. While the activity took one hour, I did not waste time listening to music. Instead, my secretary, or should I say the sultry secretary Alizeh, filled me in on the critical meetings of the day. She lived in my mansion but had separate quarters for herself. But she was supposed to join me in the gym every morning for the daily brief without fail, dressed up in a hot tracksuit and I looked forward to it, daily. I can describe Alizeh, her qualifications, looks, mischievous smile, business-like demeanor, and, most of all, figure to you in detail, but I will do it at some-other time. So after the workout, I had my daily drink of grapefruit juice and hit the shower. All dressed up, Alizeh met me at the dining table at 8.30 am exactly. That day she wore a light pink business suit, with a cream-colored shirt, matching suede sandals, a gold necklace, a smartwatch, and a light blue printed neck scarf. Man, don't ask me how hot she looked that day.

While I, the boss, rarely dressed formally, even for the most important of meetings, she was always impeccable in her dressing. Sometimes, I wonder if she did it intentionally to tease me. I don't know. Anyways, while I had two large loaves of bread, with an egg omelet filled with cheese, and a few smoked tomatoes followed by coffee, she just had plain brown bread with fresh tomatoes and a cup of tea. That explained her figure and superb physique. Breakfast over, I headed to the porch; sure enough, Zaman, my chauffeur, was ready with my sparkling BMW 7 Series Sedan all Black. Zaman has been my faithful driver for the last ten years. He is a trustworthy man and has stood by me through thick and thin.

I still remember the day I hired him ten years ago when I used to have a Suzuki Liana. And now I own a Series 7 BMW Sedan. Although this isn't the only car that I own, it most definitely is my favorite. Well, just for your information, I own a Jaguar F Type P450 Dynamic Coupe, man what a beast it is. I have an Audi e-tron GT RS, a C Class Cabriolet Mercedes Benz, and a few other cars like the Land Cruiser and a Toyota Tundra and Revo. Being a millionaire, I am accustomed to a fast-paced life. I have carved my destiny through hard work and I think I deserve it all.

So off we went to the tallest and state-of-the-art building

in the city, equipped with a Helipad on top of it. Though I can afford a Helicopter, I never did get one because I didn't feel very comfortable in a Heli, ever. An airplane, yes, of course, is another thing altogether. My Executive Secretary Sania received me at the entrance. Sania has been with me for the last five years. She is thirty-something, fair-skinned, highly educated, extremely beautiful, well-organized, endearing, very well-spoken, well-read, and alluring with the figure of a siren. Oh God! And I love her sense of dressing up. About two years ago, she stopped wearing Shalwar Kameez altogether. I think she realized she didn't look good in Shalwar Kameez, especially when we had meetings with international business partners. And I must say she made the right decision. The Western clothes, business suits, and all do proper justice to her figure. Today, she was dressed in all Blacks; WOW! I just skipped a heartbeat as she opened my car door and greeted me with her welcoming smile, shaking my hand and smiling with dimples on her cheeks. Man, I was on a roll.

The first meeting was scheduled with a group of businessmen from Japan. Well, for starters, I find the Japanese very dull; all they ever talk about is work. I wonder if there is such a word as leisure in the Japanese language or culture. How can one always be working and worrying about work? You know they smile systematically as if gauging the situation between smiles, "is it a yes or a no." Anyways work is work, I had to agree to a few of their demands, but I knew this new plant that they were willing to set up in the interior of Sind would bring me a couple of million every month. And I knew they weren't making much money out of it; they just wanted their presence in the country and to make a foothold. What did I have to lose in this all? Nothing, it was all gains for me. Therefore, after hectic discussions, and disagreements, we inked the deal with them.

Providence was shining on me; yes, it was. And then we proceeded to the next session, this time with the Germans, hell what was this day coming out to be? While the Germans were very industrious and honest, they had this innate flaw like the Japanese; they never smiled. And quite similar to the Japanese, they just worked and worked till they got tired. Anyways, this time it was about Solar energy; the Government wanted to set up a Solar Park to generate clean energy; the new policy allowed investors and people in business to set up power plants based on solar energy and sell electricity to the Government or the public. I sensed a good profit margin in this and jumped right into it. I even had a few hundred acres of land acquired for the purpose. And so we got down to discussing the intricacies of the project. While the Germans wanted a thirteen percent cut, I disagreed with it. Instead, I told them I would get them tax exemptions if they agreed to an eleven percent cut. Well, you know, I always have connections in the ruling Government and can make things work. You see, it is easier and much cheaper to buy off a few politicians and get things done your way than giving a straight two percent cut to someone in Dollars. That's where the real money is, and that's where they agreed, and eventually, we inked another big deal in one day. I could sense a few more million every month now.

While Sania and I went towards the dining hall with our German partners, I saw Alizeh coming toward me with my cell phone. I rarely carry my cell phone. Instead, I let Alizeh handle all my calls, the business ones, I mean. For private calls, I have a secret phone that I use after business hours, hehehe. You know how it goes. She told me the Minister of Industries, Syed Malik Waqar Hussian, wanted to speak to me. I have known the Minister since he was a low-level businessman until he joined a prominent political party and is now a millionaire, besides being a part-time politician. Well, they all are. So the Minister asked me if I wanted to accompany him to the US for an important meeting as part of his delegation. Well, yes, why not I said. It will be good to go with the Minister, rub shoulders with the mighty, and see the possibility of making a few good deals and making money, all at public expense.

I had a light lunch that day, just a few sandwiches and fresh pomegranate juice. After lunch, I went to my retiring room, fixed a small drink, lay on my recliner, dimmed the lights, and got the much-needed break. It was my mandatory relaxation hour. The room was on the eleventh floor, purpose-built with a high-end stereo system that played soothing music. It has a large panoramic window that gave a clear view of the city with automated blinds that operated on voice commands. Thirty minutes of relaxation with a drink in my hands, and after thirty minutes Lillie, my private masseuse, would walk in and give a much-needed foot massage for thirty minutes. That and a drink would charge me up for the rest of the day. And so, after thirty minutes, Lillie walked in with the broadest smile one could imagine and got to work. By then, I had finished my drink, and I almost dozed off while she gave me a heavenly massage. She has the softest hands anyone can have, yet her arms are strong, just like a wrestler, and she most definitely has an average figure. But I don't mind that. The massage was done in a most tranquil manner; I went to my office after that and got updates from the Finance Manager on the delayed payments from partners that were hurting my business. I called my Legal team and asked them to file suits against all defaulters. Business was business, I was a shark, and I could eat the smaller fish anytime, anywhere I wanted to. I was the master of my destiny.

The meeting was just over when Alizeh walked into my office with a smile on her face, slightly blushing; I had an inkling what she was up to. She whispered, "Sir, Ms. Sana wants to speak with you." Well, of course, you all know Sana; she is the country's most famous movie star and one of the most significant models in the fashion industry. And she's my love bird! Whenever I got a call from Sana, everyone in my office knew the protocol; they had to leave my office and let me speak to her in privacy. Sana, the dame with the sweetest voice, the cutest face, the best figure, the best curves, and all, thanked me for the Diamond necklace I had sent her as a gift last night. And yes, I also gifted her a puppy, a Pug to be exact, as at one time she had told me if she ever wanted a puppy, it would be a Pug, so a Pug it had been. And then much love talk ensued; while I talked about my upcoming trip to the US, I asked her if she would care to join me, but she politely declined, as she did not want unnecessary attention. As if the whole country did not know she was mine. But of course, you cannot reason with a headstrong woman like her. Anyways, she invited me for dinner at her place at night. Things were looking good. I wanted to take her to my farmhouse though she had been there several times, but I still wanted her to go. She loves horses, and I have recently imported a few rare breed Arabian horses for her. They are known to be the best of all. She agreed to go to the farmhouse some other day. And so, with that, the date was set for dinner at her place. I informed Alizeh to make arrangements, and sure enough, she nodded. She understands what it means when I have to go and see Sana. Alizeh was left with a few hours to prepare my clothes for the date, make a bouquet of the choicest flowers for Sana, and buy the best perfumes, dresses, and jewelry as gifts for Sana. Of course, the final decision would be mine.

That done, I called a meeting of my closest aides, which included the Manager of Administration, Finance Manager, HR Manager, International Business Head, National Business Head, Government Relations Head, and of course, my Executive Secretary Sania. Sania had changed into fresh clothes, a deep Blue business suit this time. I wonder why she changed clothes after lunch. I never asked her, but it was to entice the staff. Well, it worked for her, and I had no objections. I asked them to get me the details of the entire team working for me, the MoonStar Group, that is. I wanted to know about their families, their children, their parents, their lives, their problems, their issues, their ailments, well, almost anything and everything. And I wanted it urgently. You see, life hasn't been easy for me, and I feel I need to help people in poverty and those struggling with life.

The meeting lasted well over an hour, and everyone gave their opinion on the matter, so it ended abruptly. I wanted a coffee now, and sure enough, Alizeh sensing my mood, brought me one. Alizeh is one person who knows what I think and feel. She can almost instantly sense things and act accordingly. She plans everything concerning my welfare and comforts well in advance. And because of this, I always take her along on foreign trips with me and make her stay next to my room at the best hotels. She is close to me. I know she doesn't love me, nor do I, but then she cares for me, and I pay her well, and she's doing a fine job.

On the other hand, Sania is different; she's professional, high-grade stuff. She will never fall for my overtures; well, I know that, and she knows that I know this, so both of us play smart. But you know, I secretly fantasize about her, hehehe. Well, what do they say, boys will be boys.

After siesta, I had a meeting scheduled with the Ministry of Environment people. They wanted me to come over, but I had them come to my place instead. It was effortless to play with these people; all you had to do was invite them over for lunch or dinner, as it was well-known what kind of food we serve to our guests at MoonStar Group Head offices. I mean, the last time these people objected to the project I had just completed, and as a result, my final bill got delayed, so I had three of them flown to Switzerland, two Deputy Secretaries, and an SO from the Ministry, all expenses paid. The guise was simple; they were there to "inspect" the system I had just imported and installed at the MET Office. After that, everything went smoothly. So this time, when the proposal was floated to the Ministry for a new project by MoonStar Group, I knew what exactly to do. So during the meeting, I offered four officers an all-expense paid visit to France to "inspect" the system we were going to import and install. It was told to them that the factory was located just outside Paris, and one could see the Eiffel Tower from the factory's rooftop. Naturally, no objections were raised, and things went smoothly for me. The project was going to run smoothly, as planned. The meeting ended, and I hurried to my Penthouse on top of the MoonStar Group Head office. I had a shower, changed into fresh clothes, and fixed myself another drink. An hour later, I was on my way to Sana's house for dinner loaded with gifts. I think I dozed off on the way.

I was suddenly roused from my slumber; my mother was standing with the broom in her hand, she was wildly shaking me; I was on my charpoy, it was summer, I was drenched in sweat, and she was yelling at me, *"namurad kaam nahi karta, muft ki rotiyan tor raha hai yahan, koi thaila hee laga le."* And with that, I started my day……I dream, and I daydream quite often…..

SIFAR BATA SIFAR

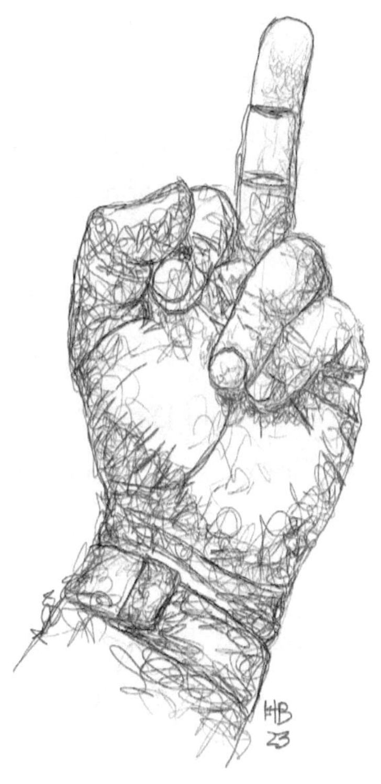

Fridays were supposed to be fun days or perhaps they were fun days. Still, in his entire service comprising over twenty years, Tahir Jamal, the energetic Deputy Director, had gotten used to getting untimely messages and letters from the "superior offices," as he used to call them. And shit would typically hit the fan between 3.45 pm till 4.30 pm, mostly on Fridays. A special messenger would arrive with a letter just about pack up time, asking for an urgent reply or data related to some pathetic five-year-old meetings' decisions, data about minorities, or data asking about the Government's past year's performance, as if they didn't know it. One didn't need to look at old files to see the Government's performance; you just had to see the latest Economic Survey or the latest fuel prices or perhaps the number of men who had died of some weird disease the past six months, or the number of women who had decided to end their lives due to domestic reasons. Therefore, when he got the letter, that particular Friday near pack-up time, the forty-two years old Deputy Director with graying hair and attractive boyish looks smiled and deep inside his heart let out the choicest cuss words for the originator of the letter. And with the same smile, he saw the file containing the letter asking for an immediate meeting coming Monday, at 11 am sharp, to discuss the Audit Paras relating to (irregularities as they liked to call them) an audit carried out eight years ago.

Tahir Jamal almost jumped out of his chair because he had for the last four years been attending similar meetings which deliberated on issues relating to the same audit paras without any outcome, and he instinctively knew this time it would not be different too. The Sarkari officers would present the points, the Audit officers would defend them, alleging gross irregularities and the Public Representatives would lambast all present about these points; the media would run tickers of it, the junior officers would take notes and make minutes of these meetings, and then the meetings would be over without any fruitful outcome. And it was because the Public representatives lacked the courage or the will to delve into these affairs and get them solved. They just wanted the media to make a day out of it and vent their anger at the Secretaries heading these Ministries. It was, as he had come to call them, "*sifar bata sifar*" meetings. Getting a letter on Friday evening meant he would have to work on Saturday for a meeting scheduled on Monday.

And so he took a photo of the letter in contravention of Government orders and sent it through Whatsapp to his boss, filling him with all the details just in time. And as expected, he got a lengthy reply asking him to spare no effort in making a detailed report for the worthy Public representatives and high Government officers. And with that, he called his clerical staff and gave them the bad news that Saturday wasn't off for them, nor him and that he would be in the office the coming day at 9 am sharp, and they better be there. With that, he packed up and left for his home. He had so many things on his mind, the top being his wife's remonstrations when she would come to know of his Saturday being a working day. Being a kind-hearted person, he had on several occasions ordered food for his staff on days they had to work that they weren't supposed to. That was his polite way of saying "thank you," and he decided to treat his staff to lunch the coming Saturday.

The following day, when he reached the office, he was happy and surprised to see his staff in the office, albeit with long faces, which he did not mind. In his mind, he imagined his face sadder and as long as a fiddle than their faces. And he smiled inwardly at this thought. And with a happy face and a despairing heart, he got down to work, instructing his staff to spare no effort in making the report, covering all the details for the information. And he got down to making a Powerpoint presentation for the meeting. Years of experience had taught him what to put in the details and what to avoid. The Secretaries did not like lots more information; they wanted just enough to cover the topic, just like a cute girl's dress, "long enough to cover the topic and short enough to be of interest." Around midday, he had some tea and some snacks. And after the Zuhr prayers, he surprised his staff with a lunch of *Pulao Kabab* and fresh fruits. They loved it and thanked him profusely. By around 3 pm, the report and the presentation were ready; he called his boss on the phone to inform him about the report and, after having sent him a copy on Whatsapp, left for his home. And so started his weekend or whatever was left of it.

Monday morning was full of commotion; it was raining, the traffic was messed up, and it was moving at a snail's pace. The Deputy Director reached the office late by a full thirty minutes. But then, everyone else was late that day; the perfect guise was provided by the heavenly rains. He got the official transport from the Motor Pool and headed straight to the venue of the Public Accounts Committee, which was to be held at the Secretariat main building Committee Room no 10. It was jokingly called by the staff "das number room". So with a complete set of files, USB drives, and laptop, the whole procession of the department made it to the "das number room." And rightly so, the "das number room," as it was called, was used for the very purposes that its name portrayed. Here the meetings of the powerful would be held regularly, and the mighty powerful, who had been fooling the public for the past seventy-five years, would rave and rant and make emotional speeches using sugar-coated words, showing empathy for the masses, whereas, there was total apathy towards the masses, their problems, and their lives. Here, a politician would get a chance to settle a score with a mighty

Secretary of a particular Ministry. The latter would, of course, say nothing in return but smile and agree to the former's accusations and menacing words, words that were not meant to bring any fruitful results but were meant to be spiteful and demeaning, giving them what they thought the others deserved right in front of everyone. On the other hand, the bureaucrats had grown thick skins, skins thick enough to withstand any ridicule or malevolence, for they knew that the politicians were powerless without them. The bureaucrats were the ones who were to stay there forever or at least till they were sixty and ready to retire, whereas the politicians were there only for a maximum term of five short years, only if they were lucky enough, that is.

That day the "das number room" was bustling with activity; there were senior officers and junior officers, and peons and clerks; in a desolate corner sat a few old men with diaries and pens in their hands, ready to take down minutes of the meetings, which over the years they had perfected as an art, using which they could with the help of a few strokes turn things into their favor or against someone else, at will. And such was the language of the bureaucracy that a particular sentence could be construed to mean two or more different things simultaneously. This was an art they had perfected over the past hundreds of years since the Goras had established the Civil Services in these regions, and the art had continued to flourish. It had passed on from one generation to another, intact and in good form. Only the conveying medium had changed from pen and paper to typewriters, and now computers and smartphones had taken over. That is what the bureaucracy had been doing since the beginning. The politicians, on the other hand, were good at lying to the public in front of them and behind closed doors, and they also had perfected the art of stealing from the public since the beginning of time. That is how Governments worked all over the world; that is how it was supposed to be, or so they thought.

Tahir Jamal handed over the USB containing the presentation to the IT guys, who, after copying it to their PC, handed it back to him, and then they did a mock run of the PowerPoint files to see if they worked or not. Sure enough, the PowerPoint file showed each slide in color and full animation mode, saying big words about the targets they had met as an organization, the excellent performance they had shown throughout the year, and the Audit objections that they had settled through "different" means. If only the data shown on the Powerpoint slides could have solved their problems, if only it were the way it was shown, if only it meant what it said, if only it were the truth, if only it did not conceal the facts, if only it did reveal the amount of money they as an organization had spent on appeasing the audit people, if only they were honest with themselves and if only they were honest with their country, if only.....

In a few minutes, the whole house was complete; there came a bevy of bureaucrats all suited booted with plastic smiles and sinister minds, then came the media people who were there to blackmail all of them, the politicians, bureaucrats, government officials, including the audit people. And finally, the Senators and Parliamentarians who were the Holiest of them all, dressed in fine suits, looking graceful, some smiling, some straight-faced, a few bearded men, a few burqa-clad women of the Islamic Alliance parties. Of course, nothing worked without alliances, and having an Islamic Alliance meant more power and acceptability in society because that is how it had been working for the last seventy-five years.

The Chairman presented his compliments to all present and introduced himself; the wily Secretary took to the microphone and asked an officer to start the proceedings with the recitation of the Holy Book. Upon that, a hush fell over the room; the few ladies with uncovered heads rolled stoles on their heads, lest they be declared the lesser of the faithful. So the meeting started with the name of Allah but against HIS teachings. From one of the Alliance parties, one funny character could not come physically and had chosen to join online through some modern IT system.

Then the audit people lamented about the sorry state of affairs prevalent in the Government organizations and, page by page, paragraph by paragraph, and word by word, lambasted and chided the Government officials for misusing public funds and causing loss to the exchequer. The chair asked the few Director Generals of an organization, and all they could reply was that they were following rules to the letter and spirit. This invited further questions by the legislators as to why the audit had observed these points when all the rules had been followed, to which the auditors replied like bare-faced liars that they had a feeling that something fishy was going on. And that they were doing an excellent service. Despite the rules being followed, a few irregularities had been observed, and one got the feeling that all the observations by the auditors had been made based on emotions instead of circumvention of rules. And in a way, it was so because, after all, the auditors were also human beings, they also had feelings, and they also wanted money and perks and cars and good food and luxury, so they carried out the audits based on their emotions.

And then the senior most politician amongst them, one with a throaty voice and an ever appeasing tone, asked a

Secretary how was that possible? And the Secretary, being a mature and sensible man, had sensed the wily machination behind the question and had instead replied to the wily politician with a twist of words, words full of malice that he would look into the matter and even hold an inquiry if needed. And at that, the politician had smiled and felt more appeased. The media person nodded in affirmative and smiled even more as he liked the mighty fighting and throwing mud at each other. So he had enjoyed it and had made a note of it in his small diary, which contained many secrets of the powerful and the rich. At that, the parliamentarian who chose to attend the meeting online went offline though everyone could hear him but could not see him when he came online and was visible, everyone could see that he was munching a samosa and drinking tea while trying to speak at the same time which wasn't possible. The senior most of them asked him to repeat the question. Then they asked the auditors why didn't they settle the issues in lower meetings and why did they have to bring everything to the Public committees and waste precious hours of the parliamentarians and thus cause significant loss to the exchequer; even the auditors were unable to answer them but had instead told them of specific rules which were framed in the late 1800s and were still suitable for implementation. And at that, the burqa-clad lady from the coalition had remarked that it was sheer negligence of the bureaucrats that laws made hundreds of years ago were still in force and that the laws needed to be amended immediately. The Secretary's immediate junior came into action and gave his valuable remarks by uttering a few sugar-coated words and strongly recommended that the committee recommend modifications in the relevant laws so that new rules could be made and to which everyone agreed. All along, the audit people remained quiet and could sense an end to their monopolistic ways, but deep inside, they knew that the laws would never be made and that things would go on working forever in the same way because that was the way it had been for the last seventy-five years. And then there arose a discussion suddenly on another point, which the audit people sensing the tide against them, agreed to settle then and there. And upon this, another firebrand parliamentarian had made a crude remark about the auditors and had rebuked them for their inadequate performance, at which everyone had preferred to keep quiet. Why could they not have settled the point earlier in a lower meeting, the man had asked, and they had had no plausible reason. The reason could never be brought to the public, not by the auditors or the Government officer who was getting all the flak. The cause was known to only two persons, the auditor, and the government officer, because he had, being a principled man, refused to get the senior audit officer's car bumper changed at his organization's expense; hence the battle had to be fought at the table with none of them having the guts, to tell the truth, and instead take support of rules and bend them if necessary.

A little while later, another largely quiet parliamentarian, after having his cup of tea, remarked why the audit points about a particular organization were over a decade older and had yet to be settled so far. There was no reply, as no one wanted to tell the reason, but everyone knew it deep in their hearts. That's why they preferred to remain silent. Of course, the point was related to some big fish, and no one wanted to invite his animosity. The Secretary sensing the direction of things and knowing well which way they were headed, decided to speak and instead told the house that he had spoken to a particular powerful minister who had agreed to resolve it on priority. So everyone agreed on this very sensible suggestion. The meeting had been stage-managed just for this reason, and the Secretary, having gotten the bait, had fallen for it, so thought the parliamentarians. But he had outplayed them all by speaking to a powerful minister beforehand and had thus shifted the blame on him, as a precaution, that is, if things ever started to go south. And at that the meeting ended with a decision to meet in three months. Sure enough, the wily Secretary would retire in precisely six weeks, and the thing would go on for a couple of years, which was his master stroke. Tahir Jamal came out of the "das number room," smiling and muttering, "sifar bata sifar."

TANIA

Talk of the town, Tania, was every boy's dream. Every bachelor officer chanted her name day and night in the garrison town of Quetta Cantonment. The fair-skinned twenty years old Tania had dark brown eyes, jet black curly hair, and was known to be a headstrong and self-willed dame. The gorgeous daughter of an Engineering Services officer was then studying in the Government Degree College, situated just outside the Cantonment. She had to leave the Cantt premises five days a week, and a bevy of young men would chase her college van from College to her house daily. Sometimes even from her house to the College, on their motorbikes with one odd car, to catch a glimpse of the girl with dimples in her cheeks. Dimples that appeared when she smiled, the same dimples that could make a man go weak in the knees and cause him to lose all sense of time and purpose. Tania, accompanied by her over-protective brother and parents while visiting the Quetta Club for weekly Tombola, could cause an incident by just looking at the boys or, worse still, by smiling at them. Many young Lieutenants undergoing their basic training at the Infantry School had, at one point or another, found themselves speechless in her presence. Under the spell of her beauty, their grades dwindled, much to the chagrin of their instructors. This was her charisma; everyone wanted to befriend her and be with her. But as far as Tania was concerned, at times, she found it difficult to even go out for an evening walk in the summers, as she would be chased by boys her age, some much older and even some young ones. She could identify most of them through their appearance and attire, but she did not know their names. So she used to call them hilarious names for her convenience. One guy amongst them was the oddest, with long incisors, long enough that she named him "kangaroo." There was a "motto," "Alam Channa," and one was simply called "handsome" by her.

Tania was not exceptionally religious, but she would say her prayers five times a day, recite the Quran daily, and was known to be very reserved in gatherings. There was no question about her beauty, which is why her father and brother had always been over-protective of her. She was not allowed to go anywhere alone, not even to her friend's house, be it Eid, birthdays, or any special occasion. In other words, it would not be wrong to say she was homebound. Hence she grew more conscious of the reason which stole her freedom: her looks! The over-protectiveness choked her at times, and constant supervision robbed her confidence, bit by bit. This all happened because of an incident that left her brother and her father in deep anger and despair. On a Chand Raat, when they returned home, they found their lawn strewn with flowers, Eid Cards, and love letters, all addressed to Tania by one of her admirers. Those were the days when mobile phones did not exist, and CCTV was unheard of. So all her parents could do was keep Tania under strict watch.

Contrary to her wishes and nature, the gentle beauty

had been forced to study Arts since no courses in Psychology, which she so badly wanted to study, were taught in her College. So, from the beginning, she had been tamed to make compromises about dressing up, going out, studying, and even choosing girls to befriend. Once a headstrong girl, she was reduced to being a docile creature. Days turned into weeks and weeks into months, until around exam time, her father got posted to Rawalpindi. An untimely posting meant she had to change Colleges just before exams. With a heavy heart, the family bade farewell to the Quetta Cantonment, their friends, and acquaintances and moved to Rawalpindi. If anything, Tania was ecstatic about the new city.

She had once lived in the city in her childhood and studied in one of those FG Schools that have lost their value in the present times. She got admission in CB College Rawalpindi, as it was famously known in those days. Left with no option, she took Arts as a subject as now she was in her final year, and exams were just around the corner. Though Psychology as a discipline was being taught at CB College, that would have meant her losing two more years. Tania was yet again compelled to make a sacrifice or perhaps was coerced. The docious girl got down to studies wasting no time and preparing for exams in the subjects she loathed to study. But that was Tania, amenable and mellow always. In time, she sat for the exams and cleared them all in one go with good grades, for she was gifted with an intelligent mind. Who said beauty and brains don't go together? She proved them all wrong.

They had been there for three months, and during that time, word got around in the Chaklala Cantonment about a certain ravishing beauty named Tania, who had just recently arrived from Quetta and was known to be a stunner. True enough, as many hearts skipped a beat when she went to the weekly Tombola on a lazy Wednesday evening with her family, to the Artillery Club, only to play a few rounds and, if lucky, to win some cash and perhaps decimate a few hearts. And Quite rightly, she did play Tombola, did not win a single rupee but did decimate many hearts. By the time they got home, around bedtime, a bevy of young men on motorbikes chased their car, and her father and brother found it hard to control their temper.

Soon after graduation, she wanted to get admission for a Master's Degree at the twin city's leading university, the Quaid e Azam University. But that was not to be, for her father being rather strict, wanted her to stay at home and help her mother with house chores. According to her father, she would be married off soon and would ultimately shoulder the responsibilities of the house as this was a woman's job or perhaps fate. With a broken heart and many tears shed in lonely corners, Tania was once again forced into giving up her dreams of further education and instead opted for house chores. Being the ever-willing girl, she considered it her fate and complied with her father's and brother's wishes.

She learned to cook, clean and wash dishes. She did the laundry, ironed her brother's clothes, and prepared meals and snacks for everyone. If there was anything she missed dearly, it was her books. Therefore, with remnant courage and lots of hope, she asked her mother for permission to go to the library once a week. Her mother coerced her father to agree, thus allowing her to go to the library once a week but, of course, in the company of her brother and never alone. The next day, Tania almost begged her brother, who reluctantly agreed to take her to the Garrison Library. She felt happy as ever, like a fish in a pond, free and cheerful. She spent much time at the library and got a few books for herself. Being a voracious reader, she soon devoured those books and yearned for more on her next visit. After house chores, she would spend time reading books and stopped watching TV altogether. Life would have continued as a beautiful dream had it not been for an ugly happening in the library. One of her paramours decided to cross the line and tried to pass on his phone number to her. This did not go unnoticed by her brother, and an altercation followed. As a result, she was prohibited from visiting the library ever again by her father. Behind the closed doors, his father consented with his brother and decided that the girl was better off married than being a liability, one that they could not shoulder for much longer.

Tania's mother was surprised at the number of marriage proposals she got for her daughter. As each proposal seemed better, Tania's mother had to seek counsel from her sisters and brothers to decide on the best groom. There were Army officers, engineers, doctors, and even a few lawyers from the aspirants. Finally, the matters ended in favor of a certain Ali Tahir, a young Lahore-based boy who had just recently returned from the USA after completing his MBA and was said to be the heir to his father's sprawling business. Her parents convinced Tania that he was a decent boy and would make a perfect match for her. Even the matchmaker aunty assured them of the boy's stock, and that his character was impeccable. After that, followed by multiple visits, Tania was betrothed to Ali Tahir, the man who would father her two kids. After her marriage, Tania underwent an ordeal that forced her to make more compromises. Compromises that were quite unnecessary and uncalled for…..

Six months later, when she got married at the relatively

tender age of twenty-one and a half, she was as carefree as a bird in most ways. Except that now she had more responsibilities, and all those house-making habits that her mother had tried to instill in her were now to be tested. But perhaps that was not the only thing she would have to do. She had to share her life with a vast family consisting of her father-in-law and mother-in-law, sisters-in-law, and a brother-in-law who was married and had two small kids. On her wedding night, her husband entered the bedroom late after midnight, drunk and out of her senses; Tania was crestfallen. That alone was a big shock for her because the demure and timid girl had never seen a man drunk except in the movies. Watching her husband in that condition on the wedding night was more than she could bear. Therefore, being a good wife and an obedient daughter, she endured his unruly and rowdy demands and antics. She was shocked, scared, and, above all, helpless. The following day, Tania woke up to some more horrors, as she found her husband to be some addict who could not regain his senses entirely until he had had his daily dose of the drug he was addicted to. When she saw her family, who came for the Walima reception, she cried her heart out. The simple folks did not know what she had gone through the previous night and ignored it.

Tania could not share her misery with them about how

she felt that particular day. Remembering the previous night's events was enough to make her throw up; the smell of alcohol and cigarette smoke was something she had never experienced before. After the Walima her parents left for Rawalpindi, and she went to her house, a sprawling mansion of sorts spread well over six kanals, and locked herself in the room. She cried bitterly and finally fell asleep. Little did she know what was in store for her. Ali would daily come home drunk and was uncontrollable in that condition. The fact that he was a drunkard and a druggie of some sort was painful enough for Tania, but what was even more unbearable was the fact that her parents had lied to Tania's family about Ali.

As a matter of fact, contrary to the realities, they had portrayed him as an ordinary being, one who was the most suitable for someone like Tania. Tania could not stop crying whenever she brooded over this fact, as she found herself and Ali poles apart in every aspect of life. She followed the rituals religiously and could not even think of the impure life that Ali was used to. While Ali was a drunkard, a drug addict, eons away from prayer and religion, and this alone was enough to make the widest gulf in their relations from day one. But Tania was compromising; yet again, she made the most significant and gravest compromise of her life because she was never given any choices. She adjusted to her situation and tried to console Ali, but he grew more aggressive with time.

The more accommodating she became; the more violent Ali became. The usual love-making sessions, or perhaps rape sessions that she called them would end in regular beatings. She would be forced to cover her marks with makeup, but at one time, a bruise around her left eye caught her father-in-law's attention, and he inquired about it. Tania tried to avoid his questioning, but all in vain, and that day she got an even more severe beating from Ali for telling on his father as if his Parents did not know of their son's antics. Just two months into her unstable marriage, she became pregnant, so her fate was sealed for worse. During the initial two months, she contemplated leaving Ali, but a Baji in the neighborhood preached that it was indeed an ungodly act, which was not liked and hence not recommended at all. Tania being the simple soul, had agreed upon fate as inevitable. With time, she gained some weight, grew a belly, and was into pregnancy; Ali became more irregular in coming home at night. He would sometimes be away from home for days, on supposedly business trips, to undisclosed locations, about which she could never ask him, nor did he feel obliged to tell her. One day, when he came home drunk and in a stupor, she laid him on the bed, removed his shoes, and put him to sleep.

While going through his wallet and other things, she found a love note in his shirt pocket, written by a certain Shumaila, with kisses planted on it in pink lipstick. From that day onwards, she started loathing the man Ali for she could not bear the thought of sharing him with another woman, and that too out of wedlock.

The next day, she walked over to her father-in-law, showed him the note, and bled her heart out in front of him. If there was one person in that house with a speck of decency, it was her father-in-law. Naturally, when her mother-in-law, sisters-in-law, and others came to know of it, they sided with their brother. Her sister-in-law went as far as to blame her for Ali's antics as being unable to satisfy his needs and wants. And when Ali came to know about the matter being disclosed, he hit her even though she was more than three months into her pregnancy and was, in fact carrying his child. She decided to end her marriage that day, but things were not going her way as her father-in-law intervened with fake promises of help. And so Tania was sent to her home for a few days until things subsided.

A week in her father's house proved tortuous for her as she was grilled by her Parents and brothers. She was asked about her sudden arrival, and having no valid reason, she told them that she missed them dearly and wanted to meet them. Being simple folks, they believed her. When she went back, things did change a little bit. She was told that Ali had to leave the country, meaning she would be alone.

Solitude gave her some respite from the physical and emotional trauma that she was going through. Days turned into weeks, Ali came back, and life went on as usual for everyone except her. Five months later, she gave birth to a lovely little girl, premature by four weeks but still healthy and alive. Ali and his family, except for Tania's father-in-law, did not seem very happy; they had been anticipating a boy, whereas Tania had birthed a girl. The baby girl was named Zuleikha, after Ali's paternal grandmother.

Two years later, Tania bore him a son, healthy and as lively as Tania herself. The boy was named Asad, this time after her father-in-law's brother, who had passed away many years ago. If anything, Tania found solace in Asad and Zuleikha. She spared no effort in their upbringing, instilling good habits and making them better beings. Everyone in the house adored them, they were the darlings, but they were also witness to the regular beatings their mother got from their father. The horrors of violence induced shortcomings in their personality and inconsistencies in their behaviors. Even a wayfarer coming to their place could make out the very unconfident look the children gave, and their demeanor was a dead giveaway.

Any loud sound, natural or man-made, was enough to send them hiding under the bed or behind the curtains. Things didn't get better for Tania, and they could not be because she had made the worst compromise ever by accepting this as fate. She sought answers to her daily misery in religion. That is why she held herself guilty when she saw her prayers unanswered with no respite. She believed it to be a way of atonement for her sins, as she might have done something terrible to deserve such a miserable punishment. And in fact, her life did not change, not one bit. Time added more years to her life, which meant not much to her, but she was living her life for her children. Ali did not change, he would not change, he could not change, she had to change, and she did change, but that only made matters worse. Ali's drinking got from bad to worse, the beatings got worse, and her life was hell. Ali started sleeping around with women half and double his age, it was a known thing, but no one could do anything about it.

One day, Tania learned about a certain office secretary of Ali's who had become intimate with him. Tania got her phone number through some of her contacts. Next, she called her and chided her. The matter got worse; she was again beaten and, on a wintery evening, was kicked out of the house. Broken, beaten, roofless and penniless, she was all by herself. She managed to get some money from a neighbor's wife and went straight to Rawalpindi, to her parent's house. Her arrival was no less than a bombshell for the entire family as they were kept in the dark by their daughter about her unfortunate life. Then began the series of frantic phone calls made by Tania's father to her father-in-law, but they didn't bear any result. In return, Tania's mother-in-law threatened Tania's parents to keep their daughter with them for good. Ali kept himself away from the scene and remained quiet. A few days later, Tania's father asked her if she wanted to end her marriage. Considering her condition and circumstances, he was willing to save her. But Tania was adamant; she told her father that she could live with abuse, beatings, marital rape, and everything, but she could never live without her kids. It was decided, and back she went to her hell hole, perhaps forever. She made yet another compromise and settled for good to submit to her husband's demands, no matter how rowdy and abusive, physically and verbally or even demeaning they were.

The young and beautiful girl with hopes and dreams, with a parade of paramours trailing behind, with looks that could bring a prince to his knees, was pitifully at the mercy of a devil. This devil ravaged her endlessly, mercilessly, and without the slightest remorse. If there was one thing she did not understand, it was that these were consequences of personal choices, always, but sadly she accepted it as her fate from providence. All Tania had to cling to was her children, and sometimes she had the flicker of hope in her father-in-law's eyes, but it was just too dim and was always overshadowed by his wife's self-willed attitude.

Things took a turn for the better, almost after a decade and a half, when Ali decided to move into a separate room forever. At least she was spared the trouble of constant abuse and ridicule. Time did not change Ali, and it did not sober him up. She had braved the storm, braved his beatings, his abuse, his mother's shenanigans, his sister's appalling behavior, and everything else in between by putting her life at stake. But she wasn't the same Tania anymore; the eyes that once glowed were now dim and at their lowest ebb. Laughter had little meaning for her; jokes meant nothing; music made no sense; food was just a means of staying alive; fashion was not to look good but to appear suitable; life was, in fact, meaningless. Her condition kept deteriorating. She became an insomniac, suffered severe back aches, and, even worse, had psychological issues that even the best of doctors could not diagnose. Ali would call her once a fortnight or sometimes a month, come to her room, they would copulate, and he would go back to his room, leaving her in a state of despair that was hard to explain and get over. She had often secretly wished for death, but owing to her deeply religious feelings, she did not pray for it. Then what? Life went on till her children reached the age of marriage.

Tania now lives in her house; both her daughter and son are married. Ali lives a few meters away from her room in the same place, in Lahore. They rarely meet, she does not miss him, but once in a while, when he needs her, she lets him have his will…Tania is still alive … .but deep inside, she's been dead for a long time. She once said to me, *"na mein kabhi chahi gai, na mein ne kisi to chaha."*

TRAGIC TALE OF RUDABA

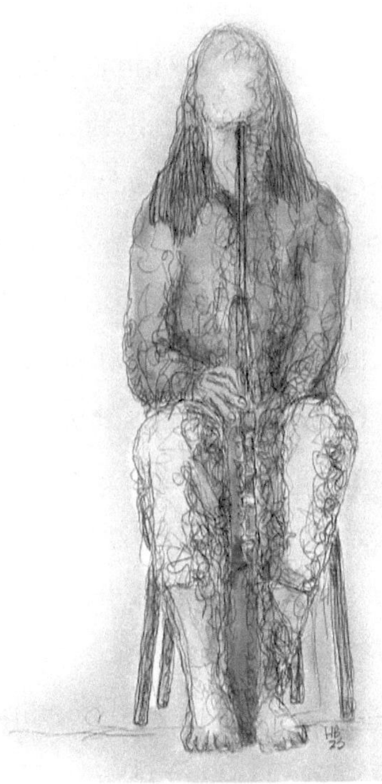

Life is fickle; hence it rarely gives us a second chance to revisit or fix our doings. Try taking it on your terms so that you may not have to live with everlasting remorse. Before continuing with life's philosophy, let me introduce myself. My name is Rudaba Tariq. I belong to a place called Sarai Alamgir near Jhelum in Pakistan. My father was a Police Officer. We were two sisters and a brother. I was the eldest, followed by my brother Raheem and then the youngest one, Tahniyat. And now, here is my story…

When I graduated from Waqar un Nisa College Rawalpindi, my father was already posted in Abbottabad as a Deputy Superintendent of Police. After the exams, I went to Abbottabad to live with my family. In those days, it was a beautiful town, peaceful, pristine, and lush green, unlike what it has become today. We lived in Jinnahabad, next to the Pakistan Military Academy. I have very fond memories of that place and those beautiful days. Our house was so close to the PMA that whenever the hooter was sounded at the beginning of the day, we could make out it was physical training time. After every forty minutes, the hooter would go on again, announcing another activity. In some ways, our lives were also synchronized with the hooter. But then, I was as carefree as a bird. My siblings were going to school and College, and I had nothing to do except help my mother with house chores or read novels. I never wanted to study more than graduation, so I preferred to stay home. We were a middle-class family, educated and decent. My father was very religious; he wanted to get me married as soon as possible. Like all parents, mine were also concerned about my future. Soon enough, I started getting proposals. Some of the proposals sounded good, but as they say, matches are made in the heavens; perhaps that is true. About six months later, I got engaged to a man named Shahzeb Rathore in the UK. My mother had asked for my consent beforehand as it was a matter of long-distance marriage. Since I was too immature to say anything, it was finalized, and I was betrothed to a man I had never seen. We began the marriage preparations which was to take place in another six months. Almost a year later, I was a married woman, hardly twenty-two years young.

My husband. a software engineer; was basically from Gujrat in Pakistan. His father had worked all his life in Saudi Arabia as a laborer and had endured great pains to educate his only son. Shahzeb had gone to study in the UK and, after that, had decided to settle down there. I saw him for the first time on our wedding day, all dressed up in a Red Gharara and Choli, right after the Nikkah ceremony when the groom was called in and as he walked towards the stage where I was seated. Just then, my bestie Zarmina had whispered in my ear, "look at him, how he's dressed up, you won't get a chance after that." Of course, it was the late 90s, and girls were still modest enough not to look or speak to their spouses on their wedding day. How have things changed now? Sometimes, I am surprised and fail to comprehend how society changes people.

Anyways, after we got married, it was my Walimah the next day, and a week later, my husband flew off to London. It took some time for the paperwork to get cleared, and after a couple of months, I joined him in London. It was the first time I had been out of the country. I was excited to be in London and, of course, to join my life partner. Shahzeb and I lived in a small apartment. Weekdays were busy for him since he would be working, so we would go out on weekends. The Pakistani community there was well-knit, and most of Shahzebs' friends had studied with him and were married then. We would socialize on weekends, and I liked the company of Pakistanis there.

During the initial period, I got close to Sumaira, who lived near our house and was married to Adnan Ahmed. Both of them were Indian Muslims. My husband was friends with Adnan, and as a couple, we got along well. A few months later, Shahzeb's mother joined us in London, and that is when my life started to change. She had stayed in Pakistan all her life, but after Shahzeb's father passed away, she decided to move to London and live with her son. She was an illiterate woman who had mostly stayed at home and had raised her kids while her husband worked in Saudi Arabia. In those times, the Internet offered dial-up connections, and calling back home was not as easy and convenient as it is today. It was expensive, and I was allowed to talk to my parents once a week. But when Shahzeb's mother moved in with us, she forbade me from calling home, saying it was costly and instead, my parents should call me from Pakistan. So, one day almost in tears, I asked my mother to call me back, and after that, they used to call me. After a year, I told my husband I was homesick and wanted to visit Pakistan to see my parents. He agreed to send me to Pakistan after getting his mother's permission. Filled with excitement, I packed my stuff and bought a few gifts for my parents and siblings. Two weeks later, I was in Pakistan.

It was good to meet my parents and siblings after a year, and I cherished every moment I spent in Pakistan. I was there for four weeks, and time passed in a flash. Four weeks later, I packed up and was again heading for London. Though four weeks is a very short time, I never knew that those four weeks would change my world and turn my life upside down. When I arrived in London, my husband seemed indifferent to me. He received me half-heartedly at the airport, said a meek "Hello," and didn't hug, kiss, or even ask about my well-being or my parents. In four weeks, he had changed tremendously. It was strange. Later, I learned that his mother had coaxed him into becoming a "real man" instead of the sissy role he was playing, that of a loving husband. I tried to ask him, reason with him, and speak to him, but he wouldn't budge. He was a different man altogether. From then onwards, a year into my marriage, we started quarreling, all thanks to my mother-in-law. At first, they were mere arguments on the most trivial of matters, such as why was not I vigilant enough to be on time for his mothers' medicines and breakfast, why wasn't her room cleaned properly, why had I shopped for more groceries than was required, etc., etc. Then those arguments would swell into shouting matches, he would throw things at me in rage, and finally came the beatings. A slap at first, a push or a shove, and ultimately hard beatings, followed by weeks of silence. Then an intermittent session of hurried sex in between, devoid of feelings from either partner; it was pure barbaric. I won't ever be able to forget that Eid Lunch which he forced me to prepare for fifty-plus guests right after my surgery that I had had in the third year of my marriage. They had removed my gallbladder. But thanks to my mother-in-law's insistence, no help was sought or asked, and I was told to do all the cooking and later clean the dishes. Sumaira did help me, but she was six months into her pregnancy, and I did not want to burden her much.

In the fourth year after my marriage, I got pregnant and

got some respite. My mother came from Pakistan to take care of me in the last stages of my pregnancy. We had met almost after three years; I burst into tears after meeting her. In a matter of hours, she could sense the negative vibes in the house. The few precise or monologue replies by my husband and the silent stares of my mother-in-law convinced my mother that things weren't normal in our home. I am particularly reminded of an incident when my mother jokingly told Shahzeb's mother that my younger sibling had asked for chocolates worth £500, to which my mother-in-law replied, "Has she ever seen £500 in real life?" Such was the level of toxicity and hatred in the house. It was beyond my understanding why they proposed for my hand in marriage if they couldn't care for me. Why do parents marry off their daughters to people they don't know? What was my mistake? Was it fate? Why is it so convenient to hate and hurt anyone rather than love or care for them? Why, but why?

After Beenish was born, I went to Pakistan along with Shahzeb and his mother for a few weeks. And those few weeks were a great respite for me. I never told my father or mother about the beatings or the ill-treatment meted out to me. I didn't want them to suffer because of me. If this was my fate, I accepted it that way. Shahzeb, I believed, found some weird sort of pleasure in teasing me as he was incredibly hostile towards my father. On that particular visit, we attended a marriage reception of one of my cousins in Rawalpindi. Shahzeb wanted to go to Lahore to buy some property. So he asked my father to drive him to Lahore. My father arranged a driver and a car for him and could not accompany him, at which he got flared up and left the place on his mother's insistence. Later, he spent the remaining days at his cousin's home and came only when we were supposed to fly back to London. After that incident, he would never miss a chance to ridicule me on the smallest of pretexts, and his mother would join the tirade, belittling me and my parents, especially my father.

My parents visited me several times in between, well, almost every year. Four years later, Zunaisha was born. When Zunaisha was three months old, my parents revisited us. They had come to London for four weeks. Before Zunaisha's birth, we had moved into a four-bedroom house on the outskirts of London. We had enough space to accommodate my parents; so they stayed with us. But then, a week after their arrival, Shahzeb argued with my father on a petty issue. He complained of a headache and rebuked my father for watching TV and not reducing the volume when told to. My father left the room. The next day again, he scolded him for drinking too much tea, which was a concocted story. I tried to reason, but he would not listen. I will never be able to forget that day. During their stay, one evening, he asked me to tell my parents to leave his house and live elsewhere. I begged him, wept, and requested him to give them a day at least to find someplace to live, but he would not agree. And so, with a heavy heart, I told them about Shahzeb's decision; my poor parents had no option but to comply. I tried arranging a hotel, but then Sumaria, as always my support, came to my rescue and offered to accommodate my parents. The same night they moved into Sumaria's place and lived there for a week, and they rented a small apartment for the rest of their stay. It was perhaps the saddest period of my life, where I would have to ask my husband's permission to go and meet my parents.

Once, Aunt Rani, who happened to be my father's cousin, came to visit me. My husband has a disliking for any of my relatives. He did not approve of any of them, and when my relatives visited me, it was a nerve-wracking experience. The stony silence, cold stares, simple monologue replies, and impolite behavior could put any honorable person to shame, except my husband and his mother. When she was still there, he got into an argument with me, which turned into a squabble, and finally, he hit me. I did not sleep in my bedroom that night and many nights after that. In fact, I preferred to sleep on the couch in the living room. Aunt Rani saw everything, and I felt terrible for myself. If this was not hell, then what would hell be like?

Two years later, my parents visited me for a few weeks. I went through great pains to convince my husband to treat them well, and thankfully he agreed but with a caveat. They would have to pay him rent daily, which he set at $25 per day according to that time. It was the most shameful thing I had ever heard. Despite that absurd proposal, my parents agreed. He took their passports three days after their arrival and counted the days they had visited us in the previous year. Later, he informed me that they would also have to pay for the earlier years in a lump sum. You won't be able to imagine how I had to go and tell my parents about that disgusting deal, get the money from them, and hand it over to my husband. They say a man is known and respected in society based on his "zarf." Shahzeb, my husband, is by all means a "kam-zarf." Sadly, they stayed for a few weeks and then left for one of my father's friends in Bristol for the rest of their stay. By now, my husband was a senior engineer in an IT firm and used to make good money. He didn't need this much money, but he did it to tease me. And his mother supported him throughout.

A few months later, his mother fell ill. In the beginning, small "essential tremors" appeared in her hands. Then it started getting worse, and even her headshakes became worse. It was perhaps divine intervention. At least I was spared the tirade daily. I was told to look after his mother, which I did, besides looking after the house. I fed, bathed, took her to the bathroom, changed her clothes, combed her hair, and even gave her daily medications. Six months later, she died, just suddenly. All this time, Sumaria, my bestie, told me to be nice to her, and I, being the straightforward woman I was, did as I was told. After her death, I thought my ordeal was over, but that was not to be. Shahzeb never forgave my parents. In fact, he is a merciless person. Very soon, he started developing a dislike for my best friend, Sumaria! At first, I did not know how to react, but then with time, I began to suspect some personality disorder in him. I spoke to a few friends, and since it was a small community, word got around, and people started avoiding us. The problem began when he suddenly started avoiding Adnan (Sumaria's husband) and decided to end his friendship with him. What were the reasons? He never told me, and I could never ask him. Then came the most significant blow when he compelled me to end my friendship with Sumaira. It was an almost two decades old friendship with my soul-sister Sumaira; and it was the most unreasonable thing he could ask for. She had been my only confidant in this alien country and in all the testing times I have been here. Parting with her was the worst thing I could do. My only support in *Pardes* would end up just like that. I tried reasoning with him, but he was adamant. No amount of pleading and coaxing worked. That is when I went to Pakistan for a few days at my father's insistence. He comforted me and assured me that, with time, things would get better. Three weeks later, when I returned, nothing had changed. The same faux pas existed; worse still, my kids had also started getting affected. They were now in their teens and could understand things. Being raised in the UK, they knew their rights and would reason with me and Shahzeb. But that man would not budge, not an inch. At last, unwillingly with great sorrow, I had to call off my friendship with Sumaira forever. A decision that I would regret later and still do.

Life got less busy, my kids were ready for university, and I had ample time. I started working at a retail outlet. With that, I could make some money which did take things off my mind. I got into a routine and made it a habit to exhaust myself physically to forget all the pain. The hardest part was staying away from Sumaria. In a small community like ours, we used to meet very frequently, and whenever I saw Sumaria at those events, it would bring back all the sweet memories and the good times we had spent together. At times, we barely greeted each other by saying, "Hello, and how are you?" I could have easily kept in touch with Sumaira without his knowledge, but I didn't want to do this. The reason is that my husband was a very suspicious kind of person. Sometimes, I even contemplated leaving him, but then I thought about my kids and our future. I could not come to any conclusion. I discussed the matter with one of my friends, who also had a very abusive husband, even worse than mine perhaps, or was it either way around, I don't know. She suggested getting professional help from a lawyer. But frankly, I never tried any of those. Instead, I would go out alone, in a park or some quiet place, and weep my heart out. It gave me comfort, especially after the forced breakup with Sumaira.

It was a cold and quiet Wednesday morning in December, and I had my day off from the retail outlet. So, after saying my morning prayers, I went to sleep. I woke up around 10 in the morning and, as a matter of habit, switched on my cell phone. There, through the message in our community group, I learned about Sumaira's death. She had gone to see her parents in Delhi and had died on the day she was supposed to fly back! My God, Sumaira, my love, she was dead. She was dead while being away from me and out of touch with me. I could not believe the fact and broke down. Having lost her, this time forever, was very painful, but the biggest regret was losing her without mending ties with her. I wished she could come back to life one more time, I would make peace with her, ask her forgiveness, and promise never to part with her. I would resume our friendship. But that was not to be. As I said earlier, life is very unpredictable and unforgiving, with consequences of our decisions. And some of them are very painful. The biggest agony for those left behind is to live a life full of regrets, and I am a living example of it!

TRANS TEMPORAL TRAVELER

My idea of being religious is rather different. I am perhaps the exact opposite of a Mullah. I believe in being honest, kind, and helpful to others. I also believe in caring for plants and animals, not hurting others. But when it comes to rituals, I am a total drab. Not that I am against it, but it's just that I am too lazy for it. Although I do pray occasionally, but when it comes to regular prayers, there is no way I can do it. I am not cut out for it. Although, I must confess my mother was a pious lady, and my father, well, I'm more like him, I guess. Besides this, I also have a few bad habits; for instance, I cannot resist an offer of a cold beer on a hot afternoon or evening. I just can't. Other than that, I am kosher! And speaking of hoarding money, well, I am not fond of it. I made good money in the electronic business. I started my company three decades ago after completing my electrical engineering from a local university. I sold fans, lights, and batteries primarily to Government offices. But then times changed, with innovation, lights got more advanced, energy savers replaced incandescent lamps, fans evolved in efficiency, and batteries gave more juice per hour. I got a big break in the mid-1990s when the country started running short of electricity. So I started selling imported generators. Everyone wanted one; it was the thing to have, the best solution for power outages. Later came those stupid uninterruptible power supplies, and now it's solar. I just kept going and getting better, and that's how I made good money in all those years. I have two houses, three cars, a small apartment in Murree, and a few shops. Life is good, and I can't complain. Now, my kids are in university, and I can afford their education at the leading universities. I call my youngest son "Junior" since he inherited my looks and is planning to go to the UK to study something called Data Science. I am lucky; I must say, very lucky, indeed.

I have a minimal social circle of four good reliable friends, myself, Junaid, Yasir and Sameen. Actually, I do not believe in having a lot of friends. It would help to have fewer but faithful friends instead of useless droves. That's my philosophy. Thankfully, all of my friends are doing good as well. Junaid is the richest of us all; he's got a good sense of property and has made big money from it. Real good money.

At times, I envy him, not because of the money but the kind of lifestyle he enjoys; it is enviable. Imagine buying the latest and best cars on New Year, going on vacations to other countries at will, living in a four kanal house with its own swimming pool, gym, jacuzzi, bowling alley, billiards, etc. Man, he's living a king's life. On top of everything, he falls for a damsel occasionally. We call him "the dirty old sod," jokingly. Last time, he almost ended up marrying a beautiful school teacher in her mid-30's. Somehow his wife got wind of it, and things started going south for him.

"The fantastic four," we call ourselves, had to intercede. Things were getting complicated. The man had lost his marbles! His eldest daughter is 19, and things do get ugly in such matters. But he was such a fantastic operator, the man just fell for it, flat! I must tell you, the lady in question was pretty; in fact, pretty would be an understatement. When I saw her, I asked myself, "Why is she even working in a school?" She could have been a top model, but you know how these things work? We tried to make our friend understand the intricacies of the whole "affair," but you know what? When men go crazy over a woman, they lose their ability to think straight. Later, we suggested that he go on a vacation and let things cool down. It worked, and he did exactly what we told him. However, in a few months, he returned to his antics running after dames. Well, all said and done, let's begin with my story.

On a winter morning, with the sun feeling good on my skin and its therapeutic warmth, I was sitting in my lawn and relaxing. There wasn't much to do that day as my wife had gone to a mall for a different kind of therapy. One that women cannot resist, "retail therapy". After having a hearty breakfast of *aloo ka paratha* and a cup of tea, I was all relaxed and in a state of trance. There was a light knock on the door which I preferred to ignore. Later, it became more pronounced and loud. Who could be knocking on the gate when he could conveniently ring a bell? I called for my faithful servant Abdul several times, but I guess Abdul was busy elsewhere.

I dragged myself half-heartedly and flung the gate open,

only to find an emaciated old man in tatters standing there. The man appeared to be in his late sixties; he had a long gray beard, wore a dark robe, and had a slipper on his left foot only. He was fair-skinned, of average height, and everything except his deep blue eyes appeared unattractive. On a closer inspection, he seemed a mendicant of some sort. With his left hand, he made a gesture and asked me for some water without saying a word. I was surprised, but of course, being the kind-hearted person I am, I went inside and fetched him a glass of water. He sat cross-legged right there on the floor, gulped down the water, wiped his lips with his right hand's sleeve, and thanked me.

Exactly then, looking towards me, he made a gesture of seeking alms. I asked how much, and he held his hands out as if saying, "ten." What could it be? I thought. Is he asking me for Rs ten or ten grand? Indeed there was nothing in between. A mere ten rupees today would mean nothing, whereas ten thousand was a mighty sum. Still, that wasn't something you got asked for on a first meeting by a stranger using gestures made by hands. Please understand my predicament. What was I to do? I went inside again and put ten rupees in my left pocket and ten, one thousand crisp rupee bills in the right one. When I came out, I saw him sitting at the same spot, and I believe

I saw the faintest hint of a smile in his eyes, for the eyes speak a different and evident language. The eyes say it all; they don't lie; I believe they are a window to a person's soul. I took out the ten rupee bill and held it to him. He stared at me for a few seconds as if saying, "are you serious" and gesticulated towards my right pocket. I was baffled; how could he have known? I wondered. I took my time and held out the ten thousand rupees to him. He accepted them readily and took out a small tin box, the kind used for keeping snuff, and handed it to me. And with that, he turned around and left. When he reached the bend of the road, at the end of the street, he looked towards me again and waved. My curiosity had, by now, got the better of me. I opened up the tin box only to find what appeared to be a few lumps of soil in it! I still cannot comprehend why I handed over ten grand to the mendicant, in fact, traded them for a few lumps of soil! Under ordinary circumstances, I would have forgotten the incident after letting off a few of the choicest expletives in my mother tongue. But this time, only this time, God knows why I just threw away the tin box and went inside. The day passed without much activity, or as they say, it was uneventful. After dinner, I had a small nightcap and dozed off around midnight.

I woke up half startled in the night, for I had seen the same mendicant in my dream, dressed in the same dark robe, pointing towards the tin box right where I had thrown it and gesturing me to eat it! What was that? I thought. Did he mean it? Was a few lumps of soil which cost me ten thousand rupees worth swallowing? Damn! I had some difficulty going back to sleep. After an hour, I woke up to the same dream with the mendicant signaling me again to eat the lumps of soil. Indeed, this wasn't normal, I thought. And when it happened thrice, I just got out of bed, donned my nightgown, tiptoed out of the room so as not to disturb my spouse, and went out of the gate. After searching for a while, I found the tin box in the bushes near my house. I walked in with the tin box, sat on the living room sofa, and gazed at the box. While staring at its contents, I was trying to decide whether to swallow one of the lumps or not.

My curiosity got the better of me, so I swallowed a small lump of soil from the tin box and washed it down with water. That done, I went to my room and, after placing the tin box in my bedside table drawer, went to sleep. I woke up amazed to find myself in a lone street, walking briskly. It was early morning. As I reached the street's end, I saw the same mendicant standing there, smiling and gesticulating at something. On a closer look, I saw an intersection with two more streets, one marked "past" and the other "future," one to the left and the other to the right. On instinct, I walked into the street that showed the sign "past." Lo and behold, it led me to a significant ground; walking past it, I found myself transported to the time when I was importing generators. My business was booming; it was perfect, but I was nowhere near the amount of money Junaid had made.

After hiring a taxi, I reached my office in an upscale part of the city. When I got there, the staff was already present in the offices. Hurriedly I walked into my office, and certainly Bina, my secretary, brought me a hot cup of tea. She was looking pretty that day wearing a bright red shalwar kameez, and the fit was banging. The red color worked well on her. I got busy at work, then the meetings started, one followed by the other, phone calls, vendors, and whatnot. Until noon, I hardly had any free time. Around a little past 1 pm, Junaid phoned me and, after the usual pleasantries, asked me whether I wanted to invest in a new housing scheme. He assured me it would make a massive profit in a short time. Junaid always had an insight into these matters. After brooding over the matter and discussing some details, I decided to invest in property instead of my line of business. I must tell you that Junaid had previously made such offers on many occasions, but I had politely refused all of them. This time with hindsight and introspection, I decided to go for it. I took out all the cash from my bank account, handed it to Junaid, and deposited the money with him after signing some papers. It was almost sundown when I returned to my office. While waiting for my usual cup of tea, I sat in my comfortable office chair and dozed off. When I woke up I was in my bed and, to my surprise, in the same era from which I had been transported. I went down to the dining room after a shave and shower. After breakfast, I reached my office and followed the usual routine. At lunchtime, Junaid dropped by unannounced into my office. It was a pleasant surprise, so we decided to have lunch in a nearby restaurant. It was after lunch that the conversation shifted to the subject of business and economy. During the discussion, Junaid reminded me of the money I had invested in plots long time ago. I was baffled after knowing the fact; how could it be? When he told me the worth of my property, I went numb. It was well over a couple of million! Quite naturally, I agreed, and then during the next few days, we sold all those plots, making a couple of millions in a short time!

I bought a brand new Mercedes car after that, a much coveted Rolex, and a new sprawling farmhouse out of the city and soon ran out of money. A week later, out of the blue, the tin box containing the loose earth lumps came into my mind. I took out a thick lump of soil, swallowed it, and drank some water. In a few moments, I was in deep slumber. Undoubtedly, I was in the same street as I woke up, with the mendicant standing at its end. This time, however, I wasted no time and walked into the road with the "past" sign. I was fully prepared as I had been transported to the past when my electronics business was booming. As previously, it was early morning when I hired a taxi to my office. After savoring the morning cup of tea served by Bina, who wore a deep blue dress, I called Junaid immediately. I intended to invest, and so I asked him for options. Sure enough, Junaid always had choices. He promptly showed me one chance in a nearby town. This time, he insisted on purchasing at least a hundred plot files. After taking the estimate, I decided to go for it, and with all the cash available, I walked into Junaid's office. Eventually, the money was invested. Later, I went to the Gentlemen's club, played a few tennis games, had a shower, and after having a few sandwiches with tea, went back to my office. The entire staff was waiting for me, for there was business to attend. But I instructed them to put everything on hold as I had had enough for the day and wanted some rest. I sat on my chair and dozed off.

Again, I woke up in my bed. This time, I was so excited to be awake in the present that I skipped breakfast and rushed to my office. I called up Junaid after having a usual cup of tea and informed him about my intention to sell properties bought a few years ago. Junaid remembered well; he asked me to visit his office along with the paperwork. You can very well imagine what happened next. That day, I made a deal worth hundreds of millions. A new investor from the UK was looking to buy a lot of property in Pakistan. They purchased my files at exorbitant rates; I made truckloads of money in a matter of weeks. Here was Junaid, my old friend who had made millions in years, and here was I, who had made more than him in weeks. There was simply no comparison between us now. I was richer than all my friends. In a few months, I bought the property in different cities, but when I got bored, I bought the property in Dubai. I invested in stocks; I bought branded clothes, my kids started going to expensive schools, and my wife got a tummy tuck, a nose job, and botox done. Although she didn't look like a queen, she sure felt like it. I bought the most expensive cars money could buy. I was on a roll. When I ran out of money, which happened sooner than I expected, in about a year's time, I went back to my old antics…

I made three more trips, and after each trip, I made more money. I was going back in time, buying property, returning to the present era, and selling it at exorbitant rates. I had more money than anyone in the entire city or the country. But I wasn't the usual show-off anymore. Instead, I kept it hidden in banks. I bought gold and kept it in banks; I bought dollars, and property, hundreds of acres of land, and I became a property tycoon. I went on foreign trips, stayed at the most expensive hotels, drank the costliest wines, partied with the best women, traveled through chartered planes, and even bought a yacht in the USA, Tampa Bay, to be exact. Life had become a joke for me; I could do anything I wanted, and I had more wealth than I could account for. But then I got bored of it.

One day, I took out the small tin box kept hidden in a vault which I got custom fitted in a wall in my bedroom. On instinct, I swallowed a lump out of it. Within minutes I went to sleep and woke up in the same street, but only this time, the mendicant wasn't there. I was all alone! Perhaps he knew I was experienced enough. That's why he left me on my own. I marched towards the street marked "past," but just before stepping in, I changed my mind and headed towards the "future". When I stepped into the street, the place was unrecognizable. It wasn't the old street I used to go to. In its place was a full metalled road with many shops and plazas. And the ground was no longer there. Instead, there was a massive building with the most modern facade I had ever seen. It was breathtakingly beautiful. Anyhow, I hailed a taxi and gave him my office address. The man literally turned around and gave me a strange look as if saying, "Are you serious?" We arrived at the place in about half an hour, and boy, was I surprised to see my office building. It was now in the most run-down part of the city.

The place had long been forgotten as outdated. I walked towards the building; a few boys were playing Cricket on the road, a dog was lazing off in the Sun, and a significantly older man, who appeared to be a watchman, was sitting on a chair. The building itself was in dilapidated condition, the beautiful entrance was not there anymore, and the company named JS Enterprises was nowhere to be seen. I approached the man and inquired about JS Enterprises, its owner, and the people who worked there. The old man examined me and remarked, *"sab khatam hogaya"*! Shocked by his words, I blurted *"khatam hogaya! Kiya matlub"*. Then the older man then narrated the most heart-wrenching story of my life…

He went into the building and brought a worn-out chair for me. He said his name was Amjad, and his father had previously worked at JS Enterprises. When I asked his father's name, he grew suspicious and asked me my name and the reason for being there. I told them my name was Tariq Ilahi and that I was a distant relative of the owner of JK Enterprises. I made up the story well; I told him I had relocated to Canada long ago and had lost contact with my dear friend. Amjad informed me that Jawed Karim had passed away many years ago, due to heavy drinking. This had led to further complications and finally taken my life.

My lovely wife was still alive and living in a small two-bedroom apartment in another part of the city. On asking about my children, well actually, I mean, the JK Enterprises owner's children, he replied that both my boys had turned against each other after my death, all because of my wealth. Despite their mother's insistence and intervention, they resorted to legal action against each other. The case had run in the Provincial High Courts for years, but no decision could be reached. Ultimately one day, my younger son was shot outside the courts. The killers were never caught, but everyone knew who was behind all this. Unable to accept the sad news, my wife lost her mind and now lived all alone.

My elder son had arranged a maid for her who cared for her. My elder son was wealthy but rarely stayed in the country. It was rumored he was a drug addict. All my friends had passed away, most of my property had been sold off, and my company had closed down. I was heartbroken in those 30 minutes or so that I spent with him and with what he told me. I was obliterated. As he went inside the building to bring tea for me, I quietly slipped out of the place and went to a nearby park. I lay down on the grass; it was a noisy place; children were playing, there was filth everywhere, and a few love birds were sitting here and there, busy in their love games. I kept thinking about the whole story, my story, the story of my life. And then I dozed off right there. When I woke up, I was in my bedroom. I got up hurriedly and looked around for my wife. She was there as usual, getting ready to go to a coffee party. My sons were still asleep. Quietly I tiptoed to their rooms and was surprised to find weird things in their rooms. Small white packets, rolled currency notes, booze, hash, and, worst of all, that odd smell.

That day, I did not go to work. I chain-smoked and thought about the future. Could I reason with my kids? I could give up drinking and convince them to quit drugs. We could still be a happy and prosperous family and be good to each other. When the boys woke up, I summoned them and asked them about what I had seen in their rooms. At first, they denied it, but then they started getting agitated. Until the elder one spoke up and said it was a trend. Surprisingly, he had the temerity to chide me about my hard drinking. Man, I was fumed, I lost it and gave them a good dressing down, but they had grown up and were more insolent. When my wife intervened, I had to let it go. I was upset. After lunch, I kept thinking about the whole affair. But then, instinctually, I took out the tin box, which had one last lump remaining. Without a thought, I swallowed it and gulped down some water. Shortly, I fell asleep, and when I woke up, I saw the mendicant there this time, in the same street. He gave me a look as if saying, "So what are you going to do?"

There wasn't much to think about; I went to the "past" this time, straight to my office, took all the property papers, and went to my friend Junaid's office without even giving him a call. He was taken aback to see me, but then I explained that I wanted to sell the property files I had once invested with him because I needed money. Junaid tried to reason with me and forbade me from selling the files. But hell no way, I said. I needed the money, and I needed it fast. So what was he to do? He processed the cases individually and found an investor who agreed to buy it at the lowest possible rates. Later he handed over the money to me. That done, I went to my bank and deposited all the money, a few million, in my account. After a hearty meal, I dozed off on my office chair.

The next day, I woke up in my bed. It was a beautiful day; I had a shower, changed into clean clothes, and went downstairs for breakfast. My wife and sons were waiting for me at the breakfast table. We chatted and laughed and had breakfast. Then the three of us, me and my two sons, went to the office together, JK Enterprises. Bina told me an important meeting had been scheduled at 11 am in the meeting room. She was wearing a jet-black shalwar kameez. Boy, did she look enticing? During the meeting, the business development manager informed them that they had received a big order for 150 KVA Generators from a Government department, a certain office in Islamabad, called the Frequency Allocation Board. While I smiled at the funny name of the department, I felt ecstatic since such a fat order would do us good and save a few million rupees. Things were looking good. The Business development manager was also happy. He told me that we had a few million rupees in the bank account and could deliver this order in weeks. I made the decision right there and then. Junaid surprised me by coming to my office. He wished me "Happy Birthday" and said, "Let's go for lunch." The good old times were back.

THE BACKSTABBER

It was a beautiful Friday morning, and Fridays are always the best days for me. That's because the weekend is just around the corner; you get a prayer break around midday, including the lunch break means at least two hours off from work and soon enough, it is pack-up time; the weekend begins, and so does the fun. But today, I had other things on mind that were far more important than just killing time the usual way. I mean, on an average day, I spend quite a bit of time on my cell phone doing Whatsapp *therapy*, therapy, yes, that's what I call it. It's almost an addiction for me now, and then there are a few things to catch up on Facebook and Instagram. And while I am at it, I make it a point to do a little bit of searching on OLX and Zameen portals, looking for things I do not need. But you know it's so much fun. And in between, I take calls, make calls, task my subordinates, chide them, give a pep talk to someone who is actually not in need of it, sign a few files, watch news headlines and have tea, lots of it. That's about my daily routine, in the office, that is, I mean. And at least once or twice a week, I visit a few colleagues and superiors in the office, get the latest gossip and then spread it to the best of my advantage and their disadvantage. I have devised this art after years of experience, and in fact, I have perfected it. I call it gossip time, but it is something else which I will tell you later…

And so after the usual cup of tea that I normally have on reaching my office, I left my office and, on instinct, strode towards the GM Administration's office. He's a nice fellow; I mean nice in the sense that he's smart and efficient and all but has no control over his tongue, and that is exactly what I use to my advantage. So I walked into Mr. Tabish Satti's office after a slight knock on the door and smilingly said, "What a beautiful day for an early morning cup of tea and some gup shup." The man stood up from his chair, greeted me with a broad smile and ordered two cups of tea. And that's when I threw in the bait, "what will happen to this country?" And Satti being the simple soul he is, took the bait hook, line and sinker. "Sir ji, I think we've lost it big time," and then his tirade started; he spoke about politicians in the vilest of words, he addressed the bureaucracy in cuss words, the establishment in even more colorful words, and finally, it was the US and Jews conspiracy he said, which was responsible for our current situation. Just in time, the tea arrived, and we got down to discussing the current issues, gulping tea and devouring a few biscuits from Tehzeeb, my favorite being those twin-colored ones, a light cream color and the brown in between. I wonder how they achieve such perfection in taste and color selection. Anyways, the talk ensued about the current economic situation, the financial bungle-ups at the highest quarters and a certain Foreign Minister who had recently visited an unfriendly neighboring country. When Satti was deeply engrossed in conversation, it was time to trap him. So I looked at him and said, "boss things aren't going to get straightened out in our lifetime at least, mitti pao." And then, just as an afterthought, I said, "How's your car?" At that, he was taken aback because he knew what I was talking about. The man had been using an official car for his family besides the one given to him by the office. After a brief pause which I believe he made to frame an appropriate reply, he said, "sir ji, it's giving me some trouble, but generally it's ok." And then he spoke about the air conditioner which broke down every few months and the overconsumption of fuel etc. But I knew he wasn't talking about the "other, unauthorized official car" that he was using but was referring to the one allotted to him officially. But who cares? I had got what I wanted to hear. And so, after some more gossip, I left his office.

Next up, I went to the GM Finance's office. He was known to be a big manipulator. He knew his job and he knew how to use things to his advantage. But then I also knew his antics well, and as I walked into his office, extending my hand, I said, *Ghazab hogaya bhai ghazab.* The GM of Finance, Mr. Faheem Anwar was no kid, but that day, he was taken by surprise; he looked up from his laptop, held my hand and asked, "Sir ji what happened?" And with the trap set, I told him about everything the GM Administration had said, including the car that was giving him problems. But I was smart enough not to mention the other car, the unauthorized one he wasn't using. And

Faheem, after using the choicest expletive in Punjabi for Tabish, said, "don't you know he's using an unauthorized car as well?" And I, being the smart one, feigned ignorance. Well, that was it, and so Mr. Faheem started with a tirade that lasted over fifteen minutes, during which he told me about inside news, about the latest happenings in the office, who was doing what and who wasn't doing what and how the public resources and money were being used, who was planning to go on a trip abroad by making use of his designation, who was using his Naib Qasid as his gardener at his home and what not.

In fifteen minutes, I had enough material to frame almost anyone in the office. And yes, this time, only this time, the smart and cunning Mr. Faheem had been cornered and taken by surprise, thus divulging important information to me. And while I took a cigarette out of his packet and lit one, I asked him a silly one, which was intended at him directly, "bhai, what will happen in the coming audit? The action on the previous one is still pending." But this alone would be used against him, as all audit matters were in one way directly or indirectly connected to his work. Faheem sensing the atmosphere, lit a cigarette and said, "sir ji, I will fix all of them, don't worry. I am more worried than anyone else." And that was all I needed to hear. Thanking him for the cigarette, I walked out of his office.

The next stop was the IT guys. They needed some fixing, and although the IT In charge was not directly a threat to me, I still wanted everyone to appear as if they had been lagging, cheating, dishonest and inefficient. That and only that, if done rightly, would mean I was the best. And in the last few years, I have proved it like that to the point that I now believe I am the best. The young IT guys were caught off guard as I walked into the Server Room with a small partition which also served as their office. A strong, sharp smell was the first thing I noticed. Hell, I knew instantly that some electric wire was short-circuited, and the plastic was burning. How could they be so dumb as not to understand and notice this? And so I stormed at them, "What's this strange smell?" All of them, actually all four of them, looked around and were dumbfounded. Off we went into the server room, and sure enough, there was a small piece of wire with smoke coming out from it and a pungent smell of plastic all around. If anything, I am grateful for it is the great sense of smell I am blessed with. Deftly the technicians were called in, the wire disconnected, the mains turned off, the wire replaced, the disaster averted, and I, the vanquished feeling elated, walked out of the IT office.

What's next, I thought? A certain old driver's brother had passed away, and I, having read the inter-office memo, decided to pay him a visit to offer my condolences. And so I went to the Transport Section looking for Driver Siddique Ahmed. He was a meek kind of a guy whom I had grown fond of, not because he could drive well or was efficient or well-mannered, but in my twenty-three years of public service, I have found drivers to be the best source of information about the Department's internal issues. These guys are amazing. They drive officers and staff around all day and quietly listen and observe everything; they are excellent snooping devices. And I did not want to lose this great opportunity of getting firsthand information from the best of them today.

The transport section was located in an unknown room of the building. A few drivers were sitting having tea or smoking in the room while one was stretched on the floor, deep asleep. As I walked in, hurriedly, they extinguished their cigarettes and stood up to greet me, excluding the one who was asleep. And so I shook hands with each of them and, looking at Siddique Ahmed, said, *"buhut afsoos hua."* And with that, all of us prayed for his brother's soul while consoling him in comforting words. After the prayers were done, I asked them about their well-being and got positive replies. One thing I must say about the proletarian class is that they are always happy regardless of the circumstances and their conditions. This upbeat mood I cannot understand or explain. And this is something we, the officer class, lack; I mean, we lack this capacity to be happy and stay that way regardless of how much money we have, the houses we have, the cars and everything. We are a thankless lot.

It was time to throw the bait and that I did by saying, *"bohat kharab halaat hain aaj kal "*. And that was all I needed to say. The men started pouring their hearts out, one by one. The first one to speak up was Siddique, followed by Abdul Kabir and then the whole lot joined in one by one. It was good to hear things about the office environments and the happenings. "The inside news," as I used to call it. For a good twenty minutes, I was provided a thorough rundown of almost all the officers, who was up to what and the commoner's perception regarding office issues, politics, promotion, salary issues and whatnot.

Armed with tons of useful information, I walked into my Boss's office with the confidence of an elephant out on a stroll in the Serengeti. The man received me with his usual smile and greetings and, seeing no file or diary in my hands, gave me a quizzical look. I knew he sensed something odd, and I immediately put him at ease, saying, "sir just wanted to say a quick hello." A seat was offered to me, and tea was ordered for the two of us. And that is when I started the session by praising him and his policies, and he felt happy at that, a smile now turned into a broad one, an ear-to-ear grin. So I started the proceedings by telling him about the GM Administration's role in the organization and how he was using an unauthorized vehicle right under the Boss's nose and complaining about the perks he was not getting. And to add fuel to the fire, I told my Boss that the GM asked about the unauthorized perks, if any, our Boss was enjoying. That sentence alone changed the grin into a frown.

The revenge on the GM was exacted. It was time to decimate GM Finance which I did by telling the Boss about the still pending replies to the Auditors. And, of course, I told him that both the GMs were scheming behind the Boss's back to make matters worse. The GM Finance knew about the GM Administration's unauthorized vehicle usage and had, in fact, cleared all fuel bills. Both were in connivance with each other and were supporting and thus opposing the Boss and his policies. The man didn't blink an eye this time. He asked for more! And I gave him more news. In one sitting, I had quashed two foes without anyone knowing. This done, I told the Boss that I had prevented a fire in the building just that day, and had I not been there in the morning, who knows, the whole office, including a few valuable lives, might have been lost. The man ordered the IT guys to be reprimanded in writing and gave me a curt "Shabash".

The day was going well for me, and that is when I asked him, "if he had heard the latest gossip?" and the man almost lost his bearings; in such times as this when he was desperate, his nostrils would quiver in unison and would present a most comical view to those present in front of him. And so his nostrils quivered, and I told him what I had heard from the drivers that morning, a rumor that the Boss would be promoted to a higher grade due to his good performance but would not be transferred and remain here in the same organization. The man in front of me, who now did not look like a boss but rather a small kid in desperation, asked me the source of the news. And I told him my sources were legit and he did not need to worry about them. And at that, he remarked, "you are amazing." And I had the gumption to tell him that a certain driver in our office had a cousin in the Ministry who was a driver with the Secretary Sahib. He had heard from none other but the Secretary's mouth regarding our Boss's promotion which everyone knew was due. Suddenly he took a deep breath and said, "I know about the promotion; in fact, everyone knows about it, but my transfer, well, this is new news." Just then, the "Azan was called, and I asked for his permission to leave, which was granted, immediately.

If you think I did anything wrong that Friday, you're mistaken. Because if I hadn't done this, someone else would have done this and beaten me at my game. Or worse still, he would have backstabbed me. I know this because I have survived in this jungle, and I know how it goes around here. It's the law of the jungle that applies here. If you don't fight, you'll be decimated and done forever. And I believe in an offensive rather than a defensive role in life. I have thus perfected the art of using my tongue to my advantage. I am a backstabber, be aware of me!

EXTENSION CABLE

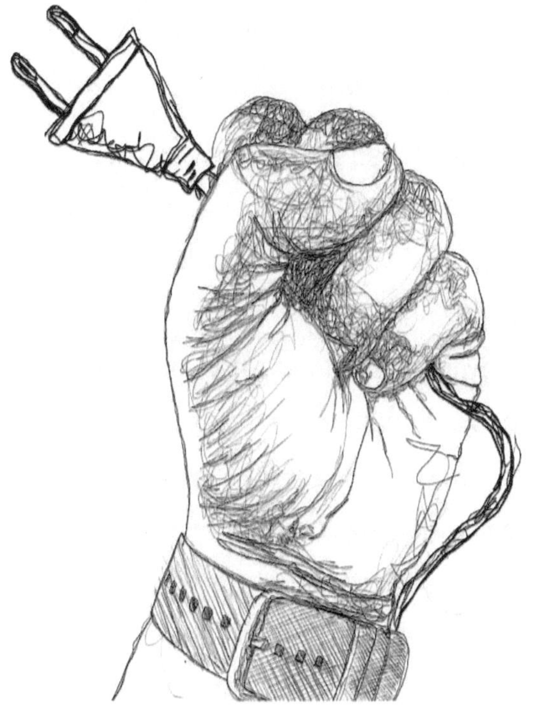

It was the third time in a fortnight that my wife had asked me to bring an extension cable for her. She wanted to attach the TV, Nayatel box and the music subwoofer to a single electricity connection. The same arrangement got its power from a UPS, and she wanted the TV to work during power outages. Being the 9 to 5 (read 5 to 9) person, I have less time during weekdays to do these chores. Therefore, on a hot and humid July morning, I cursed my fate and went to the market to get an extension board. It was Sunday, which could have been used for better things, for instance, getting a few hours of much-needed sleep, meeting my best friend, going out for brunch, or even watching a movie. But when duty calls, what else is the man of the house supposed to do?

There being few well-stocked shops in my locality, I had no option but to go to relatively far-off areas. The ideal choice would be Saddar, where you could get almost anything but the only downside was finding parking space. Even at this hour and with the punishing heat and humidity, the place was crowded with cars, motorbikes, pedestrians, shoppers, window shoppers, and young wayfarers looking for anything to appease their eyes. I switched on the data connection and searched for an electronics shop on Google Maps, of course, only after finding a desolate parking spot, one near a shady tree but with an overflowing gutter nearby. I had to decide between the stink and the much-needed shade. The shade it was! Google guided me to a nearby market that promised almost everything from cables to HDMI, speakers, USBs, printers, etc..........

The first shop had no extension cable for electricity. However, the shopkeeper said he could make one for me from local parts and that it would be ready in three days! "Three days", I said. With the Damocles sword hanging over my head, this did not sound like a good proposal to me. No way, it had to be done today or else it would certainly mean more trouble for me. The second shop had only one extension (cable), which seemed used or very old. The box containing it was dusty, the cable cracked, and the plastic almost brittle. The hot and sticky weather made things more difficult for me, I was very irritated, and I muttered some choicest expletives under my breath. What was with these guys? How could they have such big shops overflowing with unnecessary stuff except for the only item you wanted to buy? After surveying a bit, I was told to go to "Tinkoo Electronics" and meet Chacha Bhaloo. Of course, Chacha Bahloo had everything under the sun related to electricity. After giving me the directions to "Tinkoo Electronics", I noticed that the young shopkeeper smiled and nudged his comrades, and then I heard muffled giggles. The giggles turned into a guffaw as I stepped out of the shop.

"Tinkoo Electronics" was just two blocks away, and as I approached it, I had a good feeling about the shop. A big board was displayed at the entrance, with "Tinkoo Electronics" written on the top of it in bright red color over a black background, followed by "Proprietor Chacha

Bhaloo," in pink color. The shop was brightly lit, fans were running at full speed, and I could see a throng of people around the counter. While I waited for my turn, which I sensed would not come any sooner since there was no queue, I saw a much overweight man descending from stairs with a lota in one hand. He had a big paunch, and was almost bald, with big eyes and a constant smile on his face. As I looked in his direction, our eyes met, and he smiled. Assuming it to be the start of a conversation, I smiled and said, "I am looking for Chacha Bhaloo"! As the man came closer, I could sense a strange look in his eyes; they were a little bloodshot. He said, "I am Chacha Bhaloo, what do you want?" And with a heavy thud, he sat on a big revolving chair, similar to the CEO of some big multinational. Chacha took out a cigarette and lit it, then looked at me (as if saying what are you looking for?). Here is a gist of the conversation that followed…

Me: *I am looking for an extension (cable).*

Chacha: *Everyone wants an extension nowadays.*

Me: *I mean an extension for electricity, power, an extension board.*

Chacha: *Is there a difference?*

Now I was getting confused. Was the Chacha in his senses, was he kidding, or maybe stoned? Yes, the eyes were pretty bloodshot. Could he have been on some medication?

Me: *Chacha, I mean an extension for extending electricity from one place to another with multiple sockets.*

Chacha: *Electricity, hahaha, you mean power! Do you know what power is?*

Me: *Power? I mean bijli Chacha, bijli.*

Chacha: *Abay Ohm's Law, didn't you ever study Ohm's Law? Voltage is proportional to Current, Resistance being constant! And so V=IR, yaarrr, Power P=V2/I also P=I2xR, samjhay Lalloo? Ab here resistance is almost finished; therefore, we have unlimited current and lots of power, samjhay? And this unlimited power has destroyed everything.*

Me: Now, this left me agitated and restless; having studied these hateful vague formulae over 35 years ago, what was I supposed to say? Being a Doctor, I understood none of this, save for a few obscure terms. Unable to comprehend his last sentence, I said, *"Chacha Bhaloo, why don't they fix the resistance?"*

Chacha: The Chacha looked at me with a straight face and then started laughing slowly and later in convulsions. This went on for a long time until he had tears in his eyes. He stopped for breath and then laughingly said,

"Resistance is almost finished. The ones who tried always failed; now others want to increase the resistance, but the power on the other side does not let it."

Me: *Chacha, I am not getting you at all. I am talking about the factory that makes extension boards; why did they finish the resistance?*

Chacha: *Abay Lalloo, resistance is long dead. Can't you see around us?*

Me: That is when I got a sense of what the Chacha had been talking about all along.

Chacha: Taking a long puff and blowing the smoke away, said, *"Jani, everyone needs power and extension nowadays. You know what power is? It comes with an extension and you know what, extension also comes with power! In fact, if you ask me power and extension are directly proportional. Without one the other will not survive. So, it has been like this for the last 75 years.* With that, he said, *"Chal, let's solve your problem. What kind of extension do you need?*

Me: *Chacha, I need something that works.*

Chacha: *Yaarrr, you're a phudoo. How long should the wire be? How many devices do you want to connect? What will you run on it? Any particular make or brand?*

Me: *Chacha, I need something to connect the TV, speakers and Nayatel through one connection. Something durable.*

Chacha: As I uttered these words, Chacha again lit a cigarette, took an even longer puff, then, while looking at me, said, "*The best extension comes from America. It gives unlimited power, it works for years, it is guaranteed, and it doesn't malfunction till the time you don't fiddle with it unnecessarily. But it comes at a heavy price. A price we have been paying till now. Then, there is the European extension, which is unreliable because it is not guaranteed, costs less, but does give some power. Now there is a Chinese extension, it looks good on the face of it, but it is all crap. There is a Russian extension, but we never tried it. And then finally there is local extension, this is the worst kind; it needs lots of power, it is never guaranteed, and it costs an arm and a leg, but once you get it through an American company, it works as it should. So, which one do you need*"?

Me: By now, everything had fallen into place; I was clear what this seventy-plus fat man who looked stoned was talking about. Meekly, I told him, "*Chacha, I need the best one.*"!

Chacha: He laughed at me in the face, laughed some more and, taking a long puff from his third cigarette, said,

"You are all Chutias! Abay Samoo gives this sahib an American extension with five sockets, 3 USB ports and the fuse for protection."

After paying Samoo, the boy on the counter, I came out of the shop visibly shaken. As I reached home, my wife asked me, *"Extension mil gaye"*? I said, *"Yes, I got a brand new American extension."* She smiled and said, *"Shela Bhabhi was saying American extension is the best; it works for years."* Indeed, I said it works for years, and with that, I went to my room, smoked a cigarette and lay staring at the ceiling.